STARBRIGHT

STARBRIGHT

LEE MARTIN

iUniverse, Inc.
New York   Bloomington

Starbright

iUniverse books may be ordered through booksellers or by contacting:

iUniverse
1663 Liberty Drive
Bloomington, IN 47403
www.iuniverse.com
1-800-Authors (1-800-288-4677)

ISBN: 978-1-4502-4880-8 (sc)
ISBN: 978-1-4502-4882-2 (ebk)

Printed in the United States of America
iUniverse rev. date: 08/09/2010

In Memoriam

This book is dedicated to the memory of FBI Special Agent Jim Roberts, Marine, Vietnam veteran and hero to his family and friends...one of Georgia's finest. Wish I had met him.

Also by Lee Martin

The Third Moon is Blue
The Six Mile Inn
Wolf Laurel
Ten Minutes till Midnight
The Valiant

Available on Amazon.com and at booksellers

Acknowledgements

Special thanks to Vickie A. Johnson for her marvelous painting, a depiction of the character Starr Ravenel. Vickie is an acclaimed professional artist living in Suwanee, GA. Follow her on facebook, twitter and her website: www.northgwinnettartsassociation.com.

CHAPTER ONE

Summer days in Pine River can be as steamy as a pot of boiled peanuts when the blazing sun sets over soybean fields that seem to go on forever. And when the atmosphere is still and heavy, the pesky blood-sucking gnats light up from under the crops and onto the backs of unsuspecting necks and tender undersides of the arms, leaving their itchy little calling cards. There is just something about sweaty meat that attracts the minute bastards like magnets. Each day, the stillness of the coming dusk is broken at around 6:20 by the nostalgic rumble of the Amtrak in the distance beyond the fields. From the tops of sixty foot pines at the end of the perfect crop rows, obnoxious crows call and answer one another. As plain and vast as this wide open Georgia flatland is, complete with the ravenous blood-letters and sapping heat, it has its own unique and desolate beauty.

In 1982, when you're twelve and school is out for the

summer and you're biking through Farley Johnson's fields with your best friend, it is a great time to be a kid. Starr Ravenel, so named by her mother because her infant eyes twinkled and shone like diamonds against a blackboard sky on a crisp winter's night, sat with her back to a gnarly, riven pine sketching the Johnson barn. Starr was brilliant with the charcoal pencil, her work meticulously sharp in detail and dramatic with the shadows. The only renderings better than her landscapes was the human face. She could arrest the very soul in the eyes of her subjects. No one ever had any trouble recognizing the person on her sketch pad.

Starr's running buddy, Tommy Lee Bledsoe, a year her junior, propped himself against the opposite side of the tree. He eyed the burly farmer working under the hood of his black F-150 that bore the scars of a dozen years of farm use. Mr. Johnson normally didn't like anyone cutting through his field. The shortcut saved a kid a mile or more from the town proper out to 148 and Lem's Filling Station where the coldest Cokes and Orange Crushes still hung by their necks in the ancient red cooler. But Johnson was okay with Starr and Tommy Lee on his property. Starr was *Blake's* daughter and Tommy was Johnson's nephew, Katie's boy. And Blake was Pine River's Chief of Police, not to mention the Rebels' brilliant and revered High School All-American quarterback that marvelous year in Pine River football, 1968.

"So, are you coming over for popcorn and chess this evening?"

"No can do, Starr. Mom says I gotta cut the grass

before dark. With all the rain we've had, its up over my ankles. Guess I'd better get on with it."

Starr carefully finished putting the 'Y' on the roof of the barn that read **See Rock City** and without looking up, said "Won't happen. I guarantee it."

"What won't?" responded Tommy Lee.

"The grass cutting. It's going to rain in not more than half an hour."

"And how do you figure that? There ain't nothin' but white, puffy clouds up there. What are you, the dad-burned weather gal on Channel 3?"

Starr picked up a twig from the ground and twirled it between her fingers. Her expression was something between coy and condescending. "I reckon you didn't notice the black edge on the sky to the west toward Hinesville. By the time we hit Lem's and suck down a Coke, we'll be soaked."

"You ain't so smart, Starr Ravenel. You may have the entire universe sized up with that telescope of yours, but you don't know everything about the sky."

"I know we're going to have some bad storms this year. Maybe even an earthquake," she went on.

"And you know that why?"

"The planets, Tommy Boy. The planets are all aligning this year. When they line up, that affects the tide and gets our whole weather pattern off kilt. Earthquakes can also occur out in the oceans and *that* causes Tsunamis."

"Soo what?"

"Tidal waves, dodo. Huge waves that come well

into shore and flood everything out. Probably the whole east coast up to Atlanta could be wiped out. The planet alignment could even pull the Earth out of its orbit and send us spinning through space."

"Well, thank you, Suzy Sunshine," Tommy said, sarcastically. "Guess I won't need to make any more plans this year. Or the rest of my life."

"Don't be stupid, Tommy Lee. I just said it's possible. We've had other years when the planets aligned, and we're still here aren't we? Mark my word. We *will* have some very bad storms. Who knows? We may see one in just a few minutes."

Tommy Lee stood and up-righted his bike. "Betcha a dollar to a sack of farts we won't see a drop tonight."

"Well, get your buck ready, Tom Tom. We're fixing to get a good one."

Tommy Lee didn't cut the grass that evening. He not only had to cough up the buck, but was further humiliated by losing three out of four games of chess to Starr on her back porch while watching the hard rain.

The Ravenel house was a white, two-story Cape Cod built in the early 50s. Nestled comfortably under a set of oaks that were gothically adorned with Spanish moss it was flanked on one side by the Woodside's more stately Victorian and old man Kolb's run-down ranch on the other. Kolb, the weirdo.

Blake bunked in one of the downstairs bedrooms, but

the second one, the master, on the lower floor had been closed off for nearly ten years. Blake had not slept there since Starr's mother, Luann, was killed in an auto accident in early 1973 only a month after Blake had returned from Vietnam. She had apparently fallen asleep at the wheel on a Sunday night on the way back from visiting her mother in Atlanta. The Mustang had run through the wooden guardrail on the Nine Mile Bridge and plunged into Painter's Creek. The car was recovered the next morning, but Luann was not in it. Her body was found three days later nearly five miles downstream under Johnny Foster's dock. Starr was two years old at the time. As she grew up, she only knew her mother from a dozen or so photos in the family album. The photo Starr always had problems understanding was the one of her mom with a very large stomach protruding under her white wedding dress.

Starr's room was at one time an attic. Her father had refurbished it into a knotty pine bedroom that stretched almost clean across the entire upstairs. The room wasn't very deep because of the steep roofline. The ceiling dropped into the walls at a forty-five degree angle, closing off into two dormers at the front. There were two large palladium windows on either side of the upstairs, one with frosted glass over the tub in her spacious bathroom and the other at the end of her bedroom that allowed Starr's telescope to scan the heavens on vivid, moonless nights.

Pine River, in 1982, was not unlike most other Southern towns with a garden variety of shops and stores in an aging downtown area, and ancient streets lined with moss-adorned Live Oaks, flowering Magnolias and sweet blooming jasmine. It was as though sometime around the turn of the 20th Century an assembly line began producing hundreds of Confederate soldier statues for small towns like Pine River in the thirteen former Rebel states. Pine River's soldier, musket in hand, standing agelessly in the downtown square, had suffered a number of abuses over the years to include a coat of pink paint, toilet paper rollings and a broken bayonet. But for many of Pine River's citizens it was still the symbol of the 'glorious lost cause' and which proudly represented the heritage of probably seventy-five percent of the community's population.

The town, situated twenty-five or so miles south of Savannah, bumped up to the backwaters of the Atlantic and the Intercoastal toward the east and south, where watery meadows of Spartina grass or pluff mud sprawled for nearly five miles. Reeds of green and muted gold lay over the eastern landscape, softly blending land and salt water. And this summer of 1982, cotton, soon to be harvested, still clung to the branches, resembling from a distance fields of heavy frost.

Blake's father, James, was the epitome of the Southern gentleman farmer, always sporting a white Colonel Sanders style ten gallon hat and elegant manners to match. He did not grow peanuts, soybeans or tobacco like other farmers in the area. His business was milk. Blake's grandfather on his mother's side started the business. When he died at only forty-two, his daughter, young Adair Winfield, inherited it all. Adair and her new husband, James, kept the Winfield Dairy name, but everyone for twenty five years thereafter knew it as the Ravenel Dairy.

When James Ravenel died in 1964, Adair sold the dairy and bought the Cape Cod house on Jefferson Street. Adair then passed away from cancer in 1967, leaving seventeen year old Blake alone, facing his senior year in high school. But as Blake was responsible and strong in mind and emotion, and although losing both his father and mother just three years apart, he resisted successfully the county's Department of Child and Protective Services' attempt to place him in foster care until he turned eighteen. The panel took note of his maturity, ruling that he was both capable and self-sustaining. He could stay in his house and finish out school.

Standing at six-two and 175 pounds going into his senior year, Blake Ravenel was an authentic high school golden boy. By his third game that senior year he had broken the Rebels' triple threat record as a run-and-shoot quarterback in total passing yards, completion percentage and touchdowns. He had also managed the fewest interceptions in school history. By season's end, Blake had surpassed the state high school record in touchdowns and total points. His first team All-American selection did not change him, however, as he remained humble and hard-working on *and* off the field.

During his junior and senior years Blake went steady with Kathleen Hill. Katie, as she was called, was blonde, pixie-cute with bedroom blue eyes and the most popular girl in school. Avoiding the cheerleader-majorette scene, she instead concentrated on her academics, managing straight A's through her senior year. Graduating as class Valedictorian, she then set her sights on veterinarian school. Unfortunately, their romance ended after the summer of '68 when Katie accepted a scholarship offer to Iowa State.

Blake had turned down numerous football scholarships to prestigious schools such as Penn State, Nebraska and the University of Georgia. He had struggled academically at Pine River and really had no interest in college. Frankly, he didn't think he could make it through. Although he and Katie had flirted with the idea of marriage, it would just never work out. Katie made no bones about it. She wanted a college-degreed husband with drive and ambition. And Blake was merely content to work in construction with homebuilder, Harley Massingill. She did love Blake, but as she was focused on achieving financial and professional success, she kissed him goodbye in the front seat of his Mustang and threw open the door to her future. Blake didn't see her all the way into the terminal that fall day. He drove away from the passenger drop-off point without looking back.

In the spring of 1969 Blake met Luann Phillips, an attractive twenty year old lusty redhead, while grabbing a Budweiser at Lonesome Bill's out on Highway 49. Luann had moved into the area from Chicago with her dad after he and her mom divorced. She had just broken up with a boy there and as her father had been transferred to the Alcoa plant just north of Savannah, she considered this a fresh start. And it was Blake's long-time friend, Roy McIntire, whose father owned the Western Auto store in town, who immediately took up with her no sooner than she hit the area. He and Luann quickly fell into a steamy relationship that lasted two months. As much as she adored Roy, his insane jealousy and possessiveness ended their relationship. He was hot-head and more than once threatened to 'change the expression' of anyone ever looking her way.

Months later, well after her breakup with Roy, Blake began dating Luann. And that's when the two men became bitter enemies. Although each time they crossed paths, Roy fired laser beams of hate at Blake, but he knew not to start anything. Roy was strong and in good shape, but he was neither the athlete nor cheetah quick like his rival. Blake would have had Roy for breakfast.

A year later, Luann was pregnant with Blake's child and in a closed ceremony at the Presbyterian Church, they were married. The dress was white and lacey, but it was no designer wedding gown by any means. And in it, the beautiful and glowing Luann looked every bit her seven months along.

Roy McIntire's father died that year and suddenly the nineteen year old boy found himself store owner of the Western Auto. He had developed a good business head under his father's tutelage and management was an easy transition for him. But Roy didn't care for the hardware business and sold the franchise to a Savannah businessman who put up a more modern Western Auto on the south end of town. As Roy had a fascination for model cars, planes and trains, he converted his early 1900's corner shop into *Roy's Hobby Center*. Later expanding the business to include all kinds of toys, like a mini *Toys R Us*, he changed the name to *Roy's Toys*.

After her first year at Iowa State, Katie had to drop out of her pre-med studies. Her mother, divorced and alone, was diagnosed with Multiple Sclerosis and within six months found herself confined to a wheelchair. Now nearly an invalid and living only on Disability Social Security, Maggie Hill just would not be able to make it without her daughter. Katie returned to Pine River to care for her. All hopes and aspirations of becoming a veterinarian were put on hold. Maybe for good.

And so in a scant two years the lives of former lovers Blake Ravenel and Katie Hill had taken fateful turns. No one in 1968 Pine River would have ever thought it. Blake would have been a college All-American quarterback. Maybe even a Heisman candidate. But instead, he found himself married, his wife expecting, and he only making six dollars an hour building houses. Katie would not be a doctor. Sadly, she would have to take the only open job in town in 1970....waiting tables at the Kudzu Diner.

Passively despondent over finding Blake married, Katie avoided him as much as she could. When he occasionally came into the diner for morning coffee, she offered a distant smile and engaged in only small talk. Blake did take notice that she was still trim and pretty beneath the food-soiled white uniform. The long, silken hair was now pinned up and firmly secured in place by two silver combs. In his quick glances, though, he would notice how tired she always looked, as tiny, premature lines had already formed around the corners of her eyes. This came from working two full-time jobs, waitressing and nursing. The nursing was from five to seven in the morning and six in the evening until whenever her mother finally fell asleep.

Not long after Starr was born, Blake and Luann fell out over his intentions to sign up with the Army. His friends were getting drafted right and left, finding themselves six months later in Vietnam. Conservative Pine River was a bastion of blue-collar patriots, and whether Vietnam was right or wrong, the boys who were not drafted still signed up. It was the way every generation in the town had responded to wars. Even though his draft number was high, Blake felt he needed to follow his old teammates into service. Perhaps if he enlisted, he could write his own ticket. Maybe a shot at the Corps of Engineers. He would also have free life and medical insurance, be fed and clothed and would send his $200 per month allotment home until Luann and Starr could join him in his permanent assignment. Unfortunately, the recruiter had obviously lied and soon Blake was on his way to Basic Training at Ft. Polk, Louisiana, assigned to the Infantry and on orders for Vietnam. Luann was furious. Not only would he be out of her life for a year and a half, but there was that awful chance he would be lost to an enemy bullet. And where would that leave her and Starr?

Blake saw combat with the 173rd Airborne, distinguishing himself when he assumed control of his dead sergeant's squad to lead a counterattack on an enemy sapper position. He was awarded both the Silver and Bronze Star with valor, two purple hearts and promoted to Staff Sergeant. When his brigade commander colonel approached him with a battlefield commission, he respectfully declined. "The only promotion I want is to PFC, Private Frigging Civilian. And I cleaned that up, sir."

His 'Nam tour ended three days before Christmas in 1972. Blake was then released from active duty and reassigned to an Army Reserve unit at Ft. Stewart, where he was to attend monthly drills for the next year and a half.

On New Years Day in 1973 Katie Hill met a seemingly sweet and charismatic musician, Tom Bledsoe, at a party in Savannah, married him two months later, and moved her failing mother in with them. Katie then took another server position at a River Street pub, but soon found that her paycheck was supporting the three of them. Tom's 'gigs' were sporadic at best and now Tommy Lee was on the way. Their eight hundred square foot Savannah apartment just became smaller.

On January 28th, 1973, Blake Ravenel stood in a cold rain holding the tiny hand of two year old Starr as the Reverend John O'Malley put the somber finishing touches on his "ashes to ashes, dust to dust" gravesite sermonette. Starr was oblivious as to the happening and seemed more interested in plucking the petals from the white rose she held in her hand. Blake walked to his wife's coffin and coaxed the child to toss what was left of the rose onto the gravesite.

What grief he had, Blake balled up inside him and showered all his love onto Starr. It became more love than he ever imagined he could be capable. She was an easy child to love. Smart, bubbly, but ever so manipulative. Her mother had called her 'Starbright' and the name stuck. Through the years, there were only a handful of people close to her that she would allow to call her that. This was her *special* name and it was the only one and true thing her mother had left her. That, along with a spring-loaded locket that contained their photos. Luann was on the left and baby Starr on the right.

Only a year and a half after their marriage, Katie came home from the pub and found her husband Tom's note on her dresser. "Sorry, Katie. I guess I'm just not cut out for this domestic shit. Kiss Tommy Lee for me. If you ever need anything, let me know." As he had never contributed a dollar to their household income, she knew he wasn't about to start, being two thousand miles away in Canada where she learned he had joined a rock band. 1974 was not a good year for Katie all around. Her mother did not wake up one morning in early August. It was time to move back to Pine River.

Only two months after Blake started his job at the Williams Construction Company, he was out of work. With the soaring cost of new housing and the falling market, the company's losses for the second straight year were catastrophic. After failing to even meet payroll, the family gave up the business. With no other available work in town except at the city dump, it was either volunteer as an assistant coach at the high school, hoping a paying job would eventually come along, or find construction work somewhere around Savannah.

But then over a cup of coffee at the Kudzu, Orrin Tyner, who had served as Pine River's police chief since Moby Dick was a minnow, opened a dialogue with Blake about hiring on as one of his deputies.

"I don't know anything about police work, Chief. What makes you think I would be cop material?"

"Don't worry about it," Tyner replied in his characteristically gruff red-neck drawl. "I'd teach ya everything you need to know. Hell, you were one of them Ranger fellers and 'spect you can take keer of yourself. You can prob'ly teach me a thing or two when it comes to bustin' heads. And man, the folks do love you around here." He swigged a blast of coffee and ran his hand over his forehead as though he were already tired that morning. "Any way," he continued, "I won't be Chief of Police forever. Prob'ly die wearin' this badge. It won't be from a bullet, though, more like from boredom. Yore the kind of guy I'd like to see in this job one day. You could step right in when I go."

"Wouldn't Linc or Harold be in line for your job before I ever would?"

"Linc tells me every time it comes up, he don't want it. Says he's pure content with what he's doin'." Tyner then leaned across the table a foot or so from Blake and lowered his voice. "Anyway, the town council would never allow it, him bein' colored and all. Linc prob'ly realizes that and just don't want to go through the embarrassment of bein' turned down. They's still some bigotty assholes around here, boy." He leaned back and settled into his booth. "And Harold Kramer? Why he don't know anymore about depittin' than that donut layin' there. Yeah, he's been on the force for nigh on fifteen years, but he makes Barney Fife look like goddam Eliot Ness."

"I don't know, Chief. I can make two or three times the money building houses and I just can't picture myself in any kind of uniform again."

The donut and coffee wolfed down, Tyner used up the last of his sales pitch. "Just think about it, my boy. This town would love to have you and could use someone as young and bright as you on its force."

Blake chose *not* to think about it much and instead applied with two contractors, one in Savannah and the other in Richmond Hill. He was within an eyelash of accepting the job in Savannah at $10.00 per hour when the night before the day he was to begin, he sat up until three in the morning rocking a croupy Starr. As he stroked her sweet auburn hair in the quiet, dimly lit parlor, he realized that he had not considered his two year old at all in his decision. Mary Alice Baker across the street had offered to keep Starr the six days a week he was working at the rate of $2.00 an hour. But as Blake would be on the road an hour each way and likely nine to ten hours a day on the job, he would be just a Sunday father. Sure, it would only be about three years until the school system helped raise Starr Monday through Friday, but again, those were three valuable years.

She coughed herself awake and opened her sickly eyes to Blake's. No. He would never do that. Starr was all he had. His very blood ran through those precious little veins. And she was *everything*.

With some remiss, Blake accepted the town deputy position. Mrs. Baker would still look after Starr, either day or evening depending on his shift, but he would never be far away. He would somehow make a living on the twelve thousand a year.

CHAPTER TWO

On most summer days in that small, Old South village of Pine River the air was thick and dead-still, so the nauseous stench of the dumpsters in the alley behind the Bledsoe house usually did not filter through the window and into the kitchen. On this Sunday morning, however, the moist warm air that accompanied a front moving from out of the gulf, which would later spawn a thunderstorm, sent in its advance a sultry breeze that carried with it the reek of garbage that landed squarely onto Katie Bledsoe's breakfast table.

"Yech!" she exclaimed, nearly gagging. "The town has got to get these dumpsters out of the alley. I can't take much more of this." As Tommy Lee turned up his bowl and noisily sucked in the remnants of milk and soggy Trix, his mother closed the windows and touched the 'on' button on the Kenmore air conditioner that hung in the dining room window. "That is one nasty smell today.

Worse than usual. It's like a rat crawled in there and died. I'm calling the mayor first thing tomorrow morning."

Tommy, ignoring her *and* the smell, was thinking about getting up with Starr after church and biking down to Brier's Cove. These summer days, even Sundays, were all lazy, carefree and full of nothing but play and exploration. Except of course the days when Tommy had to cut the grass or wash the car. But during these school-less days there were paths to bike, backwaters to fish and ice cream to knock down at the Tastee-Freeze on Beaufort Street. Who cared about some rotten old dumpster?

Bobby Zale sat behind his desk thoughtfully mulling over the latest mugs of bank robbers, molesters, murderers and the like. He had just turned thirty the week before and a couple of deflated balloons and a black 'Over the Hill' banner still lay on the floor behind his chair. Tall and muscular with movie star looks, Bobby still resembled the athlete he was a dozen years before. He too had been a standout player for the Rebels, touted by Coach St. Clair as the 'kid with the golden hands.' Only two years after Blake Ravenel had passed for the most yards in school history, Bobby snagged more receptions and ran up more total yards than anyone before or since, leading the school to its second AAAA championship in as many years. This was Bobby's fourth year on the force. After high school he enrolled in Southern Community College to study Criminal Justice and in '73 left town for Savannah. After that, people lost touch with Bobby until he resurfaced again in 1978 when Blake, learning that Bobby had worked a while as a Savannah police officer, added him to the Pine River law team.

"Can you believe this?"

"What?" Blake asked.

"This little old lady, Mildred Clemons. She made our new flyer. Looks like she should be playing the church organ at First Baptist. Says here she's from over in King's Fork. Apparently, she stopped by her daughter's trailer and stole away her six year old granddaughter. Here's a picture of Mildred as a bank teller. Ol' Mildred found her daughter laying drunk in bed with some ex-con. It looks like she had planned the kidnapping for days. She resigned her position at the bank, withdrew her life savings and put her house up the week before."

Blake leaned over Bobby's shoulder and looked at the woman's photo. "I guess she gave up the rest of her life to see that her grand-kid would be raised in a safe and healthy environment. I know one thing: she'll be at the bottom of *my* fugitive food chain."

Bobby nodded and continued working through the flyers.

The third officer on Blake's team was fifty-three year old Lincoln Ferguson, a hefty veteran of the force best known for the ever present bag of pork rinds on his desk and his heroic capture of a violent escaped convict two years before. Linc had cornered the con in the alley behind Guy's Bar and Grill. It was a kind of standoff for a few moments. But not much of one. The con had a knife, Linc a gun. When the man lunged, Linc he did not fire. Instead, he split the man's skull with the butt end of his .45. Respected by whites as well as the community's Black population, Linc was like a father figure to Blake, always available to advise his young boss when the situation called for wisdom and experience. "Chief, my boy...," Linc would begin, but always giving Blake both his respect and endearment.

"Anything on the wire about that missing Savannah woman?"

"Just a fax, Chief," replied Linc. "Her abandoned car was found off Brunswick Road near Sundown Pond. The keys were still in the ignition and purse in the front floor. No signs of a struggle."

"Sunset Pond? That's just only a little over ten miles from town limits. Wonder what she was doing out there?"

"What every other girl does there after the sun goes down, Blake," offered Bobby. "Getting laid."

Blake continued reading. "Says she's married and has a five year old. Doesn't sound like she'd be the cheating type. Attorney. Wife. Mother. She had just left the Piggly Wiggly. Let's see. It doesn't say one way or the other whether there were groceries found in the car."

Twenty six year old Madeline Vaughan Scott was last seen the previous Wednesday afternoon. A photo of the pretty red-head was on the front page of the Sunday paper under the bold words: ***Savannah Attorney Missing. Foul Play Suspected.***

Bobby took the flyer from Blake. "Appears the GBI has divers scoping out the pond."

Blake sat on the edge of Bobby's desk with arms folded characteristically and looking out the window. "Sounds like a bad deal. My gut tells me that girl is not coming home."

"Starr?" Tommy Lee called from the front door.

"Come on up!" she yelled back.

Tommy detoured through the kitchen, grabbed an apple from the bowl of fruit on the counter top and bounded up the stairs.

Starr stood at her open palladium window peering through the 'Rear Window' lens of her telescope that today pointed downward at a 30 degree angle. As her Barlow lens brought Saturn's rings into her bedroom at night, the 26mm could pick up the wings of a bumble bee on Mrs. Potter's purple Hydrangeas across the street during the day.

"What's he doin' today?"

"I haven't seen him yet. He wasn't out on his deck all morning and all the shades are down." Starr then rotated the telescope in the direction of the house next door.

Tommy went to the window and scanned the house for himself. "His car's in the driveway. He's in there, all right."

"He gives me the creeps," Starr said. "I'll be out in the yard raking or going for the mail and there he is just standing there looking at me. He doesn't say a word. Just looks at me all mean like. Like I just threw a ball through his window or something. Then he turns and walks away, dragging that foot along the sidewalk. Clomp, scrape. Clomp, scrape. Creepy, man." She squinted her left eye and placed her right an inch or so from the eyepiece, training the telescope on the neighbor man's dining room window.

Suddenly the Venetian blind raised and the face of Rupert Kolb appeared at the window. He looked at first straight out, then raised his head and eyes slowly to Starr's palladium. Both she and Tommy Lee jumped back as though they had been shot.

"Gawd!" Tommy exclaimed. "You suppose he saw us?"

Starr nodded. "Probably. Did you see his eyes? His face looked like the Devil." She patted her chest as though that would help slow her racing heart. She and Tommy then sat down on the ancient swayback couch that belonged to her grandmother and which was later moved from the parlor to her room. Starr folded one leg under her and began tweaking her curly auburn hair. "Maybe it's about time we investigated the weird Mister Kolb."

"What do you mean...investigate?"

"Well, we know he moved here from New Jersey about three years ago. I remember Daddy had to get on him about a year afterwards for him to get a Georgia tag. And no one knows what he does, where he goes when he leaves home, and he doesn't talk to anybody. He's hiding something. Maybe hiding from the law." Starr placed her chin in her left hand and thumped her temple with the index finger. "I know! We'll go to Daddy's office and use his computer. We'll do a background check on him. I've watched Bobby do it a hundred times."

"Your dad won't let you do that! Anyway, that computer can only be used for official police business. The county library has computers."

"That's over four miles from here. I'm not biking that far. And anyway, we can't look up police files on fugitives at the library. Dad will let me on his system. I'll just tell him I'm doing some research for school."

"School's out, Einstein," sneered Tommy. "We've got two months before we go back. I believe he'll figure that one out."

"Then I'll tell him I'm looking for an article that was in *The National Astronomer.* He'll buy *that*." She scampered off 'Old Blue Velvet', as she called it, and returned to the window. "The blind's back down, now. Yep. You're a very strange dude, Rupert Kolb. And you're hiding something you don't want anyone to find out."

Linc Ferguson drove his patrol car down the alley between Williams and Darlington just before seven-thirty, making his evening rounds. As he neared the backyard of the Bledsoe house he caught sight of Katie pruning the Cassandra roses that climbed the trellis by the back porch. Hearing his car, she turned to acknowledge his approach.

"Evening, Katie!" he shouted, throwing out his hand from the driver's window.

"Lincoln," she responded with a wave of her own. "For goodness sakes, it's Sunday. Does Blake have you on shift today?"

"Yep. Since Harold retired, there're only three of us now. We gotta be two on and one off, rather than the usual two and two."

"Well, hopefully the town will approve another officer soon. Say hello to Arlecia."

Linc nodded and slowly moved on. The throaty pipes from his Crown Vic reverberated through the alley. He had scarcely cleared Katie's back gate when she saw his brake lights go on and the car jolted to a stop. He sat for a moment and then opened his door. Katie saw him stand and re-holster his night stick.

"What is it, Linc? Are you needing something?"

He shook his head 'no' and walked to the dumpster nearest her gate. After raising the lid and peering inside, he slowly closed it and reached for the control button on his shoulder-mounted radio. "Blake, this is Linc. Come in"

After a moment, a garbled voice responded. "Blake here. What's up, Linc?"

"Better come to my location, Chief. And get hold of the GBI." He paused. "*And* the M.E."

"You got trouble? Where are you, Linc?"

"In the alley behind Katie's. I think I just found the missing city lawyer."

Within minutes the entire alley was lined with official vehicles. Uniformed and civilian clad law officers from the State, County and Federal jurisdictions, reporters and curiosity seekers and others flooded the street and two or three backyards, including Katie's. It was a veritable Sunday night circus. After they all had descended on the dumpster, Blake and Linc stood buried and almost unnoticed in the sea of people watching the Georgia Bureau of Investigation's crime team gather evidence and remove the body. The description did fit the missing Madeline Scott, but it would be a day or so before the Medical Examiner made it official. The woman's throat had been cut cleanly, almost surgically, with a knife. She had been laid atop a dozen bags of garbage as though she had been posed, not dumped. She was naked and her arms were folded against her breasts formed in an 'X.' Beneath her hands was a rag doll. A Raggedy Ann doll to be exact. Blake wondered what that was about. Was the doll the killer's calling card or did it have some symbolic meaning?

He leaned his frame against Katie's picket fence. "How did you know, Linc?"

"Korea, man. That dead body smell is somethin' you don't get over. I've smelled my share of 'em and they don't smell like a dumpster full of garbage. Or any other dead animal."

Blake turned his head to where Katie sat on her back porch steps with her arms wrapped around her. When their eyes met, she shook her head sadly. Although it was still terribly hot, the chills continued to roll up and down her spine. Finally, after having all that mind and body could stand, she stood and went inside. Blake remained until the alley finally cleared of emergency personnel sometime after nine, well after the merciless sun had melted the day into night.

Murder had come to Pine River. And it had come to Katie Bledsoe's own back yard.

The next morning at about nine-thirty an agent from the GBI appeared in the doorway at the Pine River Police Department, buzzing right by Anna Mae Davenport, receptionist and part-time dispatcher. Bobby looked up from his desk to acknowledge the man who wore a dark sixties-style suit and a plain black tie. Either he was trying to look 'bureau' or he was badly in need of a GQ subscription.

"Yes, sir, can I help you?" asked Bobby, rising to his feet.

"Good morning, officer. John Lanham, GBI." He opened his coat to expose the badge clipped to his belt. "Is Chief Ravenel in?"

"He is. Go on back to his office." Bobby pointed. "That door there."

As the door was already open and upon hearing Lanham come in, Blake met him half-way. "I'm Blake Ravenel. Come on in. Did I hear you say Lanham?" he asked, shaking the man's hand.

"Agent John Lanham. Call me John, Blake."

With the pleasantries out of the way, Blake closed his door after the stocky man went before him and then lumbered his body heavily into the chair facing the chief's desk.

Blake moved toward the coffee pot. Today like every other day, the coffee was harsh and black and resembled motor oil with about six thousand miles on it. "Coffee? It's not very good. Seems like nobody in this office, not even Anna Mae out there, can make decent coffee."

"Naw, I've had my limit. Three cups. Runs through me like *Serutan*. 'Natures' spelled backwards as they say. And believe me when I say 'runs', I mean *'runs'*."

More than Blake wanted to know. "I assume you're here about the body. Reckon the coroner will confirm it was the Scott woman."

"It appears that will be the case." Lanham pulled from his coat pocket a pack of Winstons. "Mind if I smoke, Blake? I can call you 'Blake?'"

"Okay on both," He lied about the smoking. "Go ahead."

Lanham lit up and exploded a heavy plume of blue-white smoke from his lungs. Blake tried to stifle a cough.

"I need to share some things with you, Blake. Madeline Scott, if that's her, is not the first such murder in southern Georgia lately."

"What do you mean 'such murder?'"

"The thing about the rag doll. There were two other killings involving young women. Two in the past three years. Same M.O. Both had reddish hair and both found clutching one of those Raggedy Ann dolls. Obviously a killer with some kind of psycho thing going on."

"Aren't they all," agreed Blake. "I think I heard something about them. In Savannah, right? The first, maybe '79 or '80 and then a young college girl last year."

"Yeah, you heard right. The second one was a kid just out of high school who had only been married a year." Lanham took another drag, raised his head toward the florescent light and filled it with more smoke. "Summer day like this one. Her name was Carolyn Murphy. Pretty young thing. I worked her case. I don't mind telling you, it almost became personal with me. Guess I got too much into it." He sighed. "Anyway, there was talk about her messing around with some local guy. Savannah police speculated the husband found out and killed her in a rage."

"Did he?"

"Naw. I never did think so from the git go. He didn't seem like that kind of guy. Anyway, a jealous husband would probably have beat her to death rather than cut her throat like that. Again, the cut was clean and calculated, like this one and the one before. And it didn't figure to me a husband would have crossed her arms and shoved a rag doll under them. No, he passed the polygraph, and to me, appeared to be legitimately tore up over the thing."

"What about the first killing?"

"She was a socialite about thirty-two, older than either of the last two. No rhyme or reason about it. She was found in the trunk of her car, laid out naked with the doll. Had the red hair like these two."

"Any suspects in those two cases?"

"Nope." Another drag. "Stone cold, they are. Now we got *this* one. It grieves me to see these young women butchered like that. You become callused to the inner city and domestic shit, you know, but when respectable, pretty young things end up like this, makes me want to get out of the business once and for all."

Blake sat on the edge of his desk and ran his fingers over the gold frame that contained the picture of his daughter. "Why do you suppose Madeline's car was found at the pond within maybe fifteen minutes from Pine River, but her body ended up in one of our town's dumpsters?"

"No earthly idea. The socialite was found out on a desolate road near the entrance to Jekyll and the college kid on the east side of Savannah at the Montague Cemetery. Either they were stalked as targets of opportunity or got close to the killer. I figured they were somehow involved with him or at least trusted him. None of these victims showed signs of struggling. No other marks on them and no flesh under their nails."

"Were they raped?"

"Funny thing about that, Blake. Don't know about the Scott woman yet, but the first two did have recent sex. Yet there was no semen in either victim. Kind of like the killer may have had sex with them, but wouldn't go so far as to get his rocks off. Of course, nothing surprises me about these psychopaths. Maybe in some weird way he thought that would make 'em dirty. Our Psych guys have some opinions about it. One says that when the killer was a boy, his mother probably wouldn't let him play with his redheaded sister's doll. He apparently flipped out over it and now is killing women and girls that look like his mother or sister. I can't say I buy that Freudian psychobabble shit. Guess everybody with a Psych degree has some kind of slant on this thing."

"I'll be interested to see the result of this autopsy. In the meantime, we'll keep our ear to the ground. I certainly don't want to infringe upon what you guys are doing, but will go ahead and put our own investigation in motion," offered Blake.

"No problem, Chief. You know the people in this town. What you do here will be most appreciated. It can only help us at the State level. Just keep me informed. That's all I ask." Lanham searched the room for an ash tray, but not finding one, crunched out what was left of his cigarette on the sole of his shoe.

When Lanham left, Blake asked Bobby and Linc to step into his office.

CHAPTER THREE

Although now a dozen years more mature, Blake was still the mean and lean specimen of the seasoned Vietnam veteran. Or even the standout All-American Rebels quarterback. His handsome, raw-boned jaw and taut, serious mouth seldom broke out in a grin. His eyes would pierce and stare a man down, yet the chameleon pupils could turn soft and affable when it came to Starr. Always looking sharp and erect, even when a day's duty was done, his tan uniform shirt with the military creases looked as fresh as it did at six in the morning when he tucked it inside his size 32 waistband. Obviously his stomach had not seen more than one or two donuts in the past year. And his only real vice was the caffeine that came with the cup of coffee, even the office rot gut that was in his hand a dozen times every day.

That same afternoon he had met with Agent Lanham, Blake stopped off at the Kudzu for some *real* coffee before going home. Considering what had occurred not three blocks from his house, he had told Starr to stay home with the doors locked and then asked Mary Alice Baker to keep an eye peeled. And that she could. There was nothing in the neighborhood that got by her. She especially had her eagle eye on the mysterious Rupert Kolb.

After Blake slid his derriere onto the retro red and chrome bar stool, he adjusted his nightstick and Glock, then settled in with his elbows on the counter. Katie who had been on her feet since six-thirty was ready to put a wrap on her shift, but still whisked about behind the counter like a four month old kitten in preparation for the supper crowd. In less than half an hour she would be relieved by the cantankerous Minnie Ruthouse. *Nut house*, a few of the patrons called her. Who knows how much more blossoming Bennie Griffin's suppertime business would have been but for her. However, she had been serving at the Kudzu for over thirty years and was 'like furniture' around there, Bennie said. Get rid of her? Impossible. She would only go when she died. But there were some who said even that would never happen. She was just too mean to croak.

As Katie went from customer to customer, Blake watched her with eyes of a long time lover. He had taken her to bed a hundred times. In his mind. But that was back in 1968. As sweaty and breathless as they had left each other in the back seat of his Mustang at the Peach State drive-in, he had left her virginity intact. His teammates just *knew* he had tapped the hot Katie Hill, but knowing

Blake, he would be the last guy on ea[...]
about it. And no one would ever dare p[...]

When she looked back in his directi[...]
then dropped his eyes to his coffee cup. Blake and Katie
had played the cat-and-mouse game for years, long since
her divorce. They did go out a few times, however. They
had taken in an occasional movie or dinner and had even
shown up together at the Pine, Peanut and Pork festival,
slow-dancing to the country ballads sung by would-be
Patsy Clines and Conway Twittys at the end-of-festival
dance in the American Legion hall. But that was the
extent of any involvement. What he had felt in his heart
for her after high school had lain dormant for so long it
just seemed useless to think of rekindling any kind of 'for
real' romance.

Katie stopped in front of Blake and refilled his cup.
"Anything to eat tonight?"

"Naw, just the coffee. Got to get home and fix Starr's
supper. Where's Tommy Lee today?"

"Mrs. Keller is watching him this summer. She's glad
to do it now that her kids are out of the house. She loves
the company and refuses to take a nickel. I feel terrible
that she won't, so I have Tommy Lee slip a twenty dollar
bill into her money tin every now and then. She said she'd
be glad to watch Starr as well."

"Starr is fine. She's twelve going on eighteen and
mostly self-contained. She makes her own breakfast and
lunch, cleans the house, does her school work, all without
my nagging. Growing up without a mom and having a

cop for a dad, she's had to learn to be responsible. I don't worry so much and Mrs. Baker has her eye on her."

"Mary Alice Baker has her eye on *everyone* in town," chuckled Katie. "But I don't have to tell you that this is a more dangerous world we live in. Fifteen years ago no one hardly locked their doors. And now? Who would have thought in little ol' Pine River there would be a murder."

"We're not even sure she was killed around here. Could be that whoever did it, killed her somewhere between here and Savannah and just dumped her body here."

"Same difference, Blake. Still, the killer was in my back yard, for God's sake." She paused and waited for his response. There was none. "The talk is that the woman could be the victim of a serial killer. And something about leaving a doll with the bodies? That's pretty freaky and chills me to the bone. That kind of thing you might hear about happening in New York or Chicago, but not here."

Blake slowly spun his coffee cup around, looking somewhat uneasy. "Don't know if there's anything to this 'serial' stuff. Could be a copy-cat." He then threw up his hand. " Let's not go on about this anymore. The less people talk about it, the better." He stood and dropped a dollar on the counter top. Gotta get." He then took a couple of steps, but turned and looked back at her. "Am I still on your calendar for dinner Saturday night?"

Katie nodded. "Is six okay with you?"

"Six is fine. I'll bring a bottle of red."

"Make it white. We're having pork loin."

Blake smiled. She knew he loved pork loin. "Then white it is."

At the Ravenel house that evening, little was said. Blake had Madeline Scott on his mind and Starr appeared preoccupied as well.

"I saw your sketchbook on the couch, Starbright. Couldn't help but leaf through it. I hope you don't think I'm nosy or anything."

"Nope. I don't mind."

"There's really some nice work in there. I especially like the portraits. The one of Elvis looks like an honest-to-God photograph. You're on your way to becoming a really fine artist, kiddo."

Starr didn't acknowledge the compliments, but instead sat twirling spaghetti strands around her fork. "Daddy, may I ask you something?"

Blake chewed, swallowed and replied, "Sure. Ask me anything."

"What did the dead woman look like?"

"Except that," he replied.

"Somebody said her throat was cut…"

"Whoa, Starr. We're not going to talk about it. Stuff like that is not for the ears of twelve year old girls."

"I can handle it, Daddy. I'm not a child, you know. Anyway, it's been all over the TV. But I want the real stuff, not the watered-down reporter's version."

Blake laid down his fork and drilled out her eyes with his. These were not the soft, kind eyes he usually had for her. "Get all this out of your head, please, and focus on little girl things."

"Like dolls? Well then let's talk dolls. Why was the dead woman holding a Raggedy Ann doll?"

Blake banged the table with his fist. Starr had seldom seen him blow like that. As a matter of fact, not ever. Her eyes looked twice their size and she backed away a few inches from the table.

"Starr, get this and get it good! I said to forget it. Not another word about that woman. Clear?"

She put down her fork contemptuously and popped a faux salute. "Clear, Chief."

Blake glared at her a moment, shook his head and returned to his plate. After another half-hearted bite of spaghetti, supper was done.

Tommy Lee was allowed to spend the next day at the Ravenel house, because Mrs. Keller had to visit her mother at the hospice in Valdosta. Blake asked Mary Alice to check on both the children as necessary.

"He looks guilty," Starr said, staring down at the man next door. "Look. See how he digs a little around his flowers, then looks left and right like he's checking to see if someone is watching him."

They stood cautiously back from the window so as not to be detected through the glass in the morning sunlight. Rupert Kolb worked his mattock along the edge of his flower bed, deepening the trench and chopping away at the weeds.

"Looks like he's just gardenin', Starr, that's all."

"Yeah. That's what he wants everyone to think, but he's just making sure none of those bodies he's buried have washed up in the rain."

Tommy looked at Starr, half not believing, but half scared. "You really think he's buried somebody down there?"

"Maybe. Maybe he's the one who killed that woman."

"I don't know, Starr. He may be creepy, but that don't make him a killer."

"I'm not saying he is and I'm not saying he isn't. But I think it's about time we got the goods on our Mister Kolb."

After Starr and Tommy Lee slipped out the back door, they walked their bikes past the hedges in the Mollohan's yard and hit the street well out of Mrs. Baker's line of sight.

"Mom will light up my britches if she finds out I'm ridin' around today," said Tommy Lee, pumping hard and breathing heavy.

"Oh, don't be a grandma. There's no killer out there interested in snotty little boys. He likes red-headed women, remember. Anyway, we're just going to the station and there's plenty of people out on the street."

"Good morning, little ones," greeted Anna Mae.

"Good morning, Mrs. Davenport," Starr answered in almost a sing-song. She couldn't decide whether the woman looked like an old maid schoolteacher or a librarian what with Anna Mae's tight blue-white perm and sixties style glasses complete with beaded chain. She then slid into the chair by Bobby Zale's desk and began batting eyelashes playfully at him like the 1930s movie starlet she saw on the AMC channel.

"What the devil are you doing here, Starr Ravenel?" her father shouted from his office. "You and Tommy get in here."

Starr placed her hands behind her back as though she were handcuffed and bounced obediently into her dad's office. Tommy Lee followed cautiously like a puppy, scared to death of how the chief would come down on them.

Blake pointed to the two chairs in front of his desk. "Sit! You're both supposed to be at home under house arrest until I or Tommy's mom gets there. Starr, you disobeyed me today. I told you, no biking until further notice."

"Oh, Daddy. You worry entirely too much. No one's going to murdalize me. I'm too small and my hair's not Raggedy Ann red." The eyelash batting began again, only this time it was sarcastic.

Blake, who was sitting on the edge of his desk with arms folded, took a needed deep breath and exhaled audibly. Father and daughter held each other captive in a cold stare for several seconds. With his mouth tightly pursed, Blake finally spoke. "Enough," he said quietly but sternly. "I told you not to bring that up again and it's certainly nothing to joke about." He paused. "What am I going to do with you, Starbright? Don't you know I have enough on my mind than to worry about you?"

Since it was now 'Starbright,' she figured her dad wasn't going to get to the grenade stage. "I was bored at the house, Daddy, and I thought maybe I could use your computer to look up some stuff on the Witch Head Nebulae. I read an article in the *Astronomer* about it."

"Starr, I've got a lot of important, official data on the department computer and I can't take a chance on you goofing it up."

The intercom buzzed and Blake reached over his desk to press the 'listen' button. "It's Mrs. Baker, Chief," said Anna Mae's voice. "She sounds frantic."

He picked up the receiver. "Hello, Mrs. Baker. Yes, I know. They're right here. I know, ma'am. Yes. Yes. Thank you. I understand and I'm sorry. Bye bye now." He laid the receiver down slowly and looked at Starr. "You see how you've upset that woman, Starr? She's not happy at all with you, running off like that. She imagined the worst and I won't tell you what she said. At my request and out of the goodness of her heart she took it upon herself to look after you. She went across to our house, finding it empty, and panicked."

"I can't imagine why, Father dear. It's not like she found my blood all over the place."

Blake jumped up from the desk. *"Starr! Stop the nonsense right now! Another word and you'll be grounded the rest of the summer!"*

His sudden outburst shocked her, causing her to jump. Realizing he had startled her, he backed off and threw up his hand. "All right, all right. You stay right here the rest of the day until I get back. I have to meet with City Council. I mean it. Don't go out *anywhere*."

Blake walked the children out to Bobby's desk. "Sit on them, Bobby. If these desperados give you any lip, throw 'em back there in a cell."

"Roger that, Chief."

When Blake left, Starr turned to Bobby with her bright, lying smile. "Daddy said it was all right for me to do some work on his computer. Research, you know."

Bobby raised his eyebrows. "He said that?"

Tommy then looked at Starr to see how she would answer.

"Yep," Starr replied. She slid her foot over to Tommy Lee's and mashed it.

"Yeah, that's right," Tommy echoed.

"Okay, but I wouldn't have thought he'd let you be playing around on it. He's pretty particular about it, you know. Always afraid he's going to lose something."

"We'll be careful, Bobby."

Over the next two hours, Starr and Tommy Lee accessed the State and Federal law enforcement databases, putting in Rupert Kolb's name, current address, GA tag number, and then cross-indexed the information with the New Jersey State Police data bank. Similar names came up such as Ronald and Randall Kolb, and there were five mug shots with the name Kolb, none of which were of the mysterious next door neighbor. Not even a DMV record. Starr sat frustrated with the futile search. "Drats. Looks like there's nothing on him in New Jersey. It's like he didn't exist." She snapped her fingers. "Maybe he changed his name."

Bobby suddenly entered the room, seeing the New Jersey police home page on the screen. "What the hell are you all doing?"

Starr tried in vain to hide the screen with her body, placing the cursor on the 'close' icon.

"How did you get into there, Starbright? That's an official police web site."

"By watching you dozens of times."

"You know your dad would tan your hide, knowing you were into the system."

"You won't tell him, will you?"

"Not this time. But shut it down now before I change my mind." Bobby shook his head and watched as Starr hit the 'start' and 'log off' keys. "You're incorrigible, kid."

"I know. That's what makes me cute," The eye lashes started up again.

For the remainder of the afternoon she and Tommy Lee settled in on the vinyl couch that sat beneath her dad's collection of U.S. Marshal western badges reading out-dated *People* and *Newsweek* magazines.

Saturday mornings always seemed fresh and rejuvenating to the spirit, even though for kids, *every* day that school was out was like Saturday. But one could still see and feel a Saturday in the air. There were faces in town that weren't there during the work week, like farmers in their bib overalls doing their Saturday morning bank business or picking up seed and herbicides at the Co-op. After a couple of weeks had passed following the discovery of the Savannah attorney's body, things were pretty much back to normal in Pine River, although there was still a little talk about the murder here and there.

Starr was allowed back on the street and that fourth Saturday in June found her and Tommy Lee biking Old Savannah road past the Jernigan and Spence tobacco farms toward Cameron and its county library. They were the only kids in the building, because what kids in their right minds would have been seen in a library in the dead of summer, especially on a Saturday of all days.

"Mrs. Dunn," Starr began. "Would you please show me how to operate the microfiche machine?"

"Sure, honey. What are you looking for?"

"Newspapers. Papers from all over the country."

"Interesting," she replied. Mrs. Dunn then set her up behind the 'fiche' and walked her through its operation.

Starr began with the Savannah paper and read the article about the Scott woman's murder and the speculation about it having the same *motis operandi* as the two previous Southeast Georgia murders. She then scrolled back to the accounts of those 1980 and 1981 murders, especially noting the placement of the rag dolls on the bodies.

"I thought you came here to try finding something out about Kolb," said Tommy.

"Maybe I am. Is it any coincidence that he's been here three years and these murders began just under three years ago?"

"Yeah. Maybe a coincidence, but so what? That don't mean anything. There are probably plenty of people that have only been in the Savannah area three years or so. And could be someone who's lived around the area all his life did the murders."

"Okay. I'll give you that. But if he isn't the rag doll man, he's done something else. Otherwise, why isn't he in the New Jersey locator system?"

It took nearly all morning to peruse through the Newark, Hoboken and Trenton papers. Starr began by searching headlines beginning in 1980, then day by day, worked backwards. All the way back to 1965, where she suddenly stopped. Her heart leapt and raced as she zeroed in on a photo of a man seated on a sofa beside his wife and two girls. The man's face seemed all too familiar to her and she punched Tommy Lee in the arm with her knuckles.

"God-a-mighty!" he exclaimed, rubbing his bicep. "What did you do that for?"

Starr put her index finger on the man in the photo. "Who does that look like to you? Maybe a younger version, fifteen or so years. It's him."

Tommy studied the picture and the headline above it: "*Woman, Two Daughters Murdered. Man disappears.*" "Am I supposed to believe that's Rupert Kolb?"

"Don't you think it looks like him? Think younger."

Tommy Lee squinted his eyes and shrugged.

"It says all three had their throats cut. The husband's shoe print was found in a pool of his wife's blood. His closet was cleaned out and the family car missing. No wonder Kolb acts like he does, always looking around like he's afraid someone is watching him. He's been on the run. His name was Stanley Morris back then. Daddy's got to see this, Tommy Lee. He's the one all right. Looks like he's back to his old murderous ways." She then printed out the article from August 13, 1965 as well as others that ran in the Trenton paper for several days after.

Starr pulled her bike onto the front porch about four, finding her dad home and in his room. He was standing in front of the dresser mirror combing his wet hair, making faces and scrunching up his nose. With an index finger he matted down an unruly eyebrow. He then heard the giggle behind him.

"You're primping. You're actually primping."

Blake, a bit embarrassed, reacted defensively. "Get out of here, Starbright. I'm not primping, okay? Can't a guy groom himself without his daughter sneaking up on him? Get cleaned up, kid."

"Why do I have to clean up? I'm not going anywhere."

"'Fraid so, sweetie. We're going out to supper."

Starr looked thoughtfully at the ceiling and put her index finger playfully on her forehead. "Oh, dear. Could it be? No. This wouldn't be a date with… *Katie Bledsoe*?"

Blake spun Starr around and smacked her gingerly on the butt. "Apparently, you've been talking to Tommy Lee. Now get up there and change. *We* have a date at six."

He turned back around to check himself out in the full length mirror. He did look rather GQ in his starched khakis, black knit Tee, Navy blazer and weejuns.

CHAPTER FOUR

Blake and Starr arrived at Katie's, finding the aroma of baked pork loin and peach pie blending together for an olfactory delight. As Starr scampered off to Tommy's room, Blake set the Riesling down in a bucket of ice on the bar and stood with his posterior against the sink. Katie wore a sleeveless top that served to broadcast the deep cleavage between her ample breasts. Her skirt had the shine of silk and clung tenderly to her shapely thighs. It all tended to arouse Blake's libido enough to where he had to cast his eyes out the window to focus on something other than Katie Bledsoe. The eyes found the dumpster not fifty feet away that scarcely two weeks before had contained the bloody body of the young Savannah attorney. Seeing the dumpster again was indeed enough to change his mood.

Katie saw him looking at the huge, green metal box. "It'll take me a good while before I ever walk out to that dumpster again," she said. "Every time I look at it I get sick to my stomach. Just to imagine, a psychopathic killer this close to my house."

"Try not to think about it, Katie. Just be thankful you're safe. The guy's probably long gone and I doubt he'll ever set foot in Pine River again."

Katie didn't look at him and continued putting the silverware and plates on the dining table. "What makes you think he doesn't live right here in this town?"

"I think it was happenstance, Katie. The other killings were over in the Savannah area…" He then took her hand to stop her busyness. "Let's…just change the subject. I came here to eat, you know, and I'm starved."

Starr had brought with her the print-outs from the Trenton newspaper shoved inside her sketchbook. While her dad and Katie were talking, she was in Tommy's room putting the finishing touches on a free-hand sketch of the face in the news photo.

"He must have been a monster to kill his family like that," she remarked, applying shading, wrinkles and bags under the subject's eyes. "The article said Stanley Morris was a church-going man who worked for a Trenton accounting firm. Guess all those figures and formulas running through his head one day caused him to snap. I know *Algebra* drives *me* crazy, not that I would ever end up killing anybody over it though." She gave Tommy a sinister look. "Not yet, anyway."

She completed the portrait, laid her pencil down and

held the pad out in front of her. As she had seen a police artist do at a GBI convention that she went to with her dad, Starr aged Stanley Morris by giving him wrinkles, a sagging face and a balding head. "What do you think, Tommy Lee? Is that Rupert Kolb or what?"

Tommy squinted his eyes as though it would somehow allow the sketch to take on the likeness of Starr's neighbor. "Maybe. I reckon it looks a little like him all right. But he also looks like Mr. Warren, you know, the guy at the bank."

"Oh, damn, Tommy Lee," Starr said in a huff. "You wouldn't be able to recognize a dump truck if it ran over you."

From downstairs they heard Katie calling. "Supper's on the table! Wash up and come on down!"

Blake noticed Starr picking at her food. "Eat up, Starr. You don't want Katie to think you don't like her dinner, do you. You look like you're a million miles away."

"I'm just a deep thinker, that's all. I can't help it if my brain is so huge that it fills up with more stuff than the average human being's does. It's a real burden being so much smarter than other people, you know."

Blake shot a quick glance in Katie's direction and rolled his eyes. Katie choked a little on her string beans and giggled while sipping some water.

"Starbright," Blake began. "I don't know what planet you zipped here from, but I'm sure it was from a galaxy far, far away."

They all laughed.

Starr's eyes then took on a serious look as she laid down her fork. "Daddy, I've got something to tell you. Katie, it's okay for you to hear this too, especially since you and Dad are an item."

Blake cleared his throat, looked quickly over at Katie and then down at his plate.

"Could be I've solved the murder of that woman in the dumpster. And if not this one, maybe the murders of a family up in New Jersey."

"What in the world are you talking about?" Blake responded. "I told you..."

"Wait, Dad. Hear me out." Starr ponied up in her chair, straight and confident. "It's our neighbor, Mr. Kolb. I'm pretty sure he's a murderer."

Blake leaned back, heaved a sigh and shook his head. "Starr, Starr" he said quietly. "Why would you say such a thing? I know you think he's a kook, but so are half the people in this town. I suppose you have some evidence to back that up?"

From under the table Starr pulled out her sketchpad. She opened it up to reveal an extremely vivid, almost professionally sketched likeness of a haggard-looking gentleman perhaps sixty. She then dropped beside her father's plate the news article. "See? It's him. He is the guy who killed his family."

Blake glanced down at the material and turned his head to Katie. "Have you ever...?" Then with resignation, he picked up the article and began reading. Starr thought at first he would be all over it as he appeared to be studying the news clipping with an immense degree of thoughtfulness.

Blake settled back again and rested his elbows on the table, hands clasped under his chin. "You haven't let anybody see this, have you, Starr?"

"No. I just copied the news article today and drew Mr. Kolb a few minutes ago."

Blake leaned into Starr. The expression on his face said it all. "Okay, listen up, little girl. You tear up this stuff and I mean tonight. You are not to further speculate, investigate or tell anyone else this fairy tale. Do you want me to get sued for slander or libel? That's what will happen if you spread this…this crap around town about Mr. Kolb. Now tell me you'll forget all about this nonsense."

Starr bit her bottom lip. As she had never heard *this* kind of ire in her father's voice, it was as though some alien had entered his body. Eyes round and glossy, she replied softly. "Yes. But Daddy…"

"No 'buts', Starr. You heard me."

"Okay," even softer.

Blake then sat back in his chair. The father-daughter scene had made the supper atmosphere uncomfortable.

"Excuse me," Starr said quietly, pushing back her chair. She fired a dart with her eyes at her dad and left the room.

Katie who had been silent during the admonishment spoke up. "Blake, I know what you said was right, but look at the sketch again. This is as good a drawing as anything you'll see in a courtroom. It does look a little like the man. And here, look at the news article. Could that be a younger Kolb?"

Tommy Lee added his two cents. "Yeah. I didn't think so at first, sir, but the more you look at it…"

Blake interjected. "Now don't *you* all start up about this. Look. You know what kind of vivid imagination Starr has. She could see the Virgin Mary in a bowl of Alpha Bits. If there was anything to this, don't you think I'd be all over it? Let's just let this thing die, okay? Starr will get her nose back in joint and then be sure to stick it into something else."

Katie gracefully laid her napkin by her plate and smiled. "I'll go see about her. Why don't you bring the pie out, Tommy Lee? Be right back."

Starr came back down for dessert after Katie's visit. She and her dad didn't talk nor did they much look at one another. Although the room was not frozen, there was still a chill in the air.

After supper was cleared away and the children returned to Tommy's room for a game of chess, Blake retrieved the sketchpad from the dining chair and placed it by his keys on the hall table. As he laid it down, he shook his head and whispered 'Starr.'

The creak in the hall floorboard behind him only momentarily preceded the soft voice. "She's a sweetheart, Blake. Don't be too hard on her. She may be irrepressible, but she's charmingly irresistible as well. Kind of like her father. And I just love her spirit. And she's right, you know."

"About what?"

"She is so much smarter than every other kid around here. Melodramatic, audacious, formidable? Yeah, that's Starr. And… I do agree you need to keep her in check; but be careful not to break her spirit."

Blake nodded and locked eyes with her. The corners of his mouth almost turned up into a smile.

"Come on, Chief. Help me with the dishes."

"Sure. Want another glass of wine? I'll pour."

"That would be nice," she replied sweetly. "But you're still helping with the dishes."

As she began soaping the plates, Blake threw the dishtowel over his shoulder and poured out two glasses.

Tommy Lee had put Starr in check with his bishop in less than fifteen minutes. She was definitely not on her game. And he was not sure in the dim light of his nightstand lamp…but her cheeks appeared moist. "Are you crying?"

"Of course not."

"So you still fumin' about your dad jumpin' on you?"

Starr pushed the board away. "I don't get it. My dad's the police chief. And a good one, everybody says. So why doesn't he see what I see? Just because I'm his daughter and twelve years old, I guess anything I have to say doesn't matter."

"Yeah, but Starr, you got no proof. You can't go around accusin' somebody without proof."

"You don't think the article and my picture aren't enough proof? It all adds up. The guy moved here from New Jersey about the same time the first two murders were committed. If he killed his family, maybe he couldn't stop killing. It got into his blood like an addiction or something. Maybe his wife was red-headed and she nagged him to a point where he couldn't take it any more. Now every time he sees a red head, he reacts like when a bull sees a red cape."

"Damn. You sure *do* have some kind of imagination, all right," said Tommy, shaking his head.

"Well thank you for your support, Benedict Arnold."

The dinner dishes done, Blake and Katie took their half full glasses into the living room. While he plopped into the vinyl sofa chair, she took out a short stack of 45s and dropped them onto the spindle of her ancient turntable. When the needle met the vinyl, the crackle followed and soon the tender voices of the Vogues coated the room like warm honey.

"Don't get too comfortable there, Slim," she said, turning down the three way lamp to 25 watts. Katie took him by the hand and gently pulled him up from the chair. She swung him into her and began the slow-dance. "Remember this? It was one of our songs."

There is someone walking behind you. Turn around, look at me....

Their torsos touched as they swayed and rocked slowly with the music. This was the same Katie of their teens, yet her body now felt mature. Her movements were calculated and graceful, not that she was just a bubble gum chewing, bouncy live wire at eighteen. But she was now svelte and sensuously magnetic. He guessed that was the difference between girl and woman.

"Why did you wait so long, Blake?"

"What do you mean? Wait so long for what?"

"You know. Us. I know you needed some time after you lost Luann, but why nine or ten years of going out of your way to avoid me?"

"We *have* gone out a few time times, you know. And where do you get the idea I've avoided you?"

"If you call a couple of socials, a few movies and dinner at the *Skylark* going out, okay. But…"

"And you were expecting we'd pick back up where we left off in high school."

"Maybe. But maybe I thought you would at least show me something of the Blake I used to know."

He didn't respond and his silence seemed to amplify the lyrics.

…and there's someone to love and guide you. Turn around, look at me.

"I thought about it. Then I thought how much water was over the dam and how you and I were not the same people we were back then. I…I really didn't know how we could pick it back up. Or if it would ever work out if we did."

Katie had been holding her wine glass in her left hand and left arm draped over Blake's shoulder. She took a sip, finding the liquid warm and biting. She then returned her forearm to his shoulder, causing the glass to touch his ear. She smiled and sighed.

"What?" Blake asked with a reciprocating smile. He actually smiled.

"I came across a picture of us the other day. It was when we went to Myrtle Beach right after we graduated. You had just bought that 68 Mustang. I can see us now barreling up Highway 17, you thinking you were Steve McQueen, all cool and in control. Remember when we entered the shag contest at Studebaker's? If they had given a trophy for last place, we would have won hands down. God, you were an awful dancer." She sighed again. "I miss who we were."

"I miss that Mustang," he chuckled.

Katie released her right hand from his left and pinched him hard on his buttock.

"Ow! What was that for?"

"For nothing, Blake Ravenel. Ten years of nothing."

Oh, I've waited, but I'll wait forever. For you to come to me. Look at someone who really needs you. Turn around, look at me.

The vogues ended their ballad and a new 45 dropped. Now it was James Taylor and *Something In the Way She Moves*.

Katie glued her eyes onto Blake's. "Ever wonder if I hadn't gone off to college and you hadn't taken up with Luann, where we'd be?"

"Probably more times than you would think. I was hurt when you left, Katie. At the time, I felt like you may as well have run off with another guy the way you left it. But you know what? I did something I never thought I'd ever do. I got over you."

"I guess you did, considering by the time I got back to my mom, you were already married. Was what we had not strong enough for you to wait till I was out of college?"

"How could I know that if you did finish out, you'd set up practice back here. I wasn't about to follow you clear across country to wherever. I let you know that my roots are here in this town with these people." He took his eyes off hers and looked aimlessly around the room.

"So that's the reason all this time you've hardly looked in my direction. You were still stewing about my leaving? I had no idea you harbored all this inside you."

Blake turned his head back to her. "No anger, Katie. No hard feelings. Probably more apathy than anything."

More silence. The music, though low, practically hurt their ears.

"So why are you here tonight?"

His eyes worked over her face. She was beautiful, all right. Now maturely beautiful. Every sensual movement of her lips screamed for him to taste them. But he wasn't ready. Not yet.

"Maybe the apathy has run its course. Maybe it's time to chart a *new* course."

Another one of their oldies dropped from the spindle. It was the Casinos sweet ballad, *Then You Can Tell Me Goodbye.*

Blake ran his hand along Katie's back and up under her blouse, savoring the silken skin. His fingers slid along the valley of her spine, up and down, finally stopping at the top of her skirt. Finding the zipper, he dropped it down a half dozen teeth until he touched nylon. That was far enough. There were two children in the house. He returned the zipper to where he found it.

Katie leaned her head to the side of Blake's face, touching his sandpaper cheek. His lips had found her neck at the jugular just below her ear. His hot breath sent chills though her spine. Even though her loins burned and ached with desire for him, her mind told her that this was futile, even wrong. The love they had fourteen, fifteen years ago was dead, buried in the crevices of their memories. They weren't the same fresh and innocent kids they were in 1968 Pine River High School. Even though her body had been so starved for love over the years, she had not let herself think about bedding down with anyone. That is, except Blake. But on their handful of dates, there had been no after-dinner, after-movie sparks.

As thoughts and memories continued running through their heads, they hadn't said much to one another for moments on end. Finally, Blake picked it back up. "Guess I never told you this. And I have no idea why I'm telling you now." He paused, smiled and shook his head. "Naw."

"What?" Katie said, grinning and positioning his head with her forefinger on his chin. "Go ahead. Spit it out."

Blake, still smiling uncharacteristically, looked away as though he were embarrassed. Then he continued. "I remember the first time we kissed. Oh, I had kissed a ton of other girls.....even Jennifer Burton who was a ton all by herself. But yours...damn. It was like kissing a fresh breath of air that filled my lungs so full, it took my own breath away."

"Why Blake Ravenel. You're a certified romantic. That was…poetic."

And now he *was* embarrassed.

Katie gained control of his eyes with hers, parting her lips slightly and then working over his like moist velvet. She teased him by drawing back and flashing her perfect white teeth beneath the patented Katie Bledsoe smile. Her eyes were radiant, even glistening in the soft light. "And does that still take your breath away?"

He smiled again, not having to say a word.

As she swayed with Blake to the music of another time, Katie was at last experiencing something that felt very much like love again. She let the now empty wine glass fall softly onto the carpet and touched her fingers to his temple, sweeping the dark hair back to his crown. She again moved her lips over his cheek and onto his mouth. The wine on his lips tasted warm. They breathed into each other as one, sucking passionately, ravenously.

Then they heard the giggles. Through the stair railing peeked the two small faces of their children. It wasn't that they were making fun of their parents; they were just delighted to see them together like that. It was something that Starr and Tommy Lee had wanted for a long time.

Starr climbed into the front passenger's side of the Blazer as her father slid under the steering wheel. She then ran her hand along the stock of the twelve-gauge that was locked against the instrument panel.

"Eh, eh! You know not to touch that," chided Blake.

"Will you teach me how to shoot one day, Daddy?"

"Some day, Starr. But not with that. The recoil will knock you on your keester."

She was quiet for a couple of blocks, but then as her dad turned into their driveway, she broke the silence. "I'm sorry, Daddy."

"About?"

"About the Kolb thing. Maybe you're right. He's probably just another crotchety old man who hates kids. Guess that's why I thought he'd make a good candidate for a murderer."

Blake stopped the engine and stroked the back of her head. "I just want you to make good decisions in your life, Sweetie. It's not that I don't believe you. Whether you're right or wrong, just know that I believe *in* you. But when it comes to crime-solving and catching bad guys, that's *my* job, okay?"

She nodded.

"I love you, Starbright, kooky kid and all." He kissed her on the forehead. "Now go on in and get ready for bed. I'll come up and say goodnight in a while. Got to check in with Linc."

CHAPTER FIVE

Only moments after the last elements of light faded from the early summer sky, a golden full moon began its climb up the northern horizon over Lake Coowatchee. Its soft radiance did not take long to brighten the landscape, convert to a brilliant silver and spread its shimmering rays upon the lake water. Coowatchee, a relatively small lake, was a favorite recreational venue for early morning anglers…as well as late night lovers.

Marcia Rose St. Clair, Marcie, as everyone knew her, had wanted to go with her friends from her 1982 graduating class to Daytona the first week of June, but instead spent four days in the hospital with a mild case of viral meningitis. Daytona was to be the spring board for their special summer and the 'ultimate event.' She and Jake Thigpen had been flirting for three months with going all the way, but she had made sure that their dates had ended up with nothing more than a little groping and fondling.

Marcie was every guy's dream girl: Homecoming Queen, head cheerleader, and bombshell, the cause of many a nocturnal emission... *but* also the coach's daughter. And the latter was the reason none of the hunks on the Rebels' squad would ever ask her out. They would pay dearly with pain and sweat if Coach ever found out.

Jake Thigpen, however, was no athlete. Although a wiry, good-looking kid in a greasy sort of way, he was not very popular with other classmates. His shoulder length slicked-back hair and Marlboro suspended loosely from his lips in James Dean fashion did not exactly make him a social magnet. Most of the girls thought he was kind of cute, but steered clear, speculating he would end up like his old man: serving time in the State Penn. And then, Blake Ravenel had caught Jake along with two other boys from nearby Cabbagetown breaking into a Coke machine. Rather than arresting them, he drove each boy to his respective home, chewed out the parents and told them their next stop next time was 'juvy' if there was any more trouble. Blake also knew Jake's mom would beat the boy half to death within minutes after his Blazer pulled out from the trailer park and that would be punishment enough. No way would her boy end up like his father.

Marcie's mom knew her daughter was seeing Jake and although she didn't particularly like the boy, she didn't forbid Marcie to go out with him. There was a lot of whispering and eye darting between the two women as they were careful to keep Marcie's little fling a secret from

Coach. But there were still words of caution from Beulah St. Clair in any event.

Perhaps ten yards from shore they waded into the lake until its gentle waves lapped over their shoulders. The night was to be their 'Daytona' since Marcie and Jake had missed Beach Week. The water felt warm, even oily to their naked skin. The young lovers, kissed, teased and pursued one another playfully, then passionately. They were out just far enough for the smaller Marcie to touch her toes on the murky bottom and keep the water level below her chin. Jake gobbled her lips and dunked his head under to tantalize her nipples with his tongue.

Through a row of scrub oaks the unseen figure crouched low so as not to be reflected in the ever brightening moonlight, watching Marcie and Jake feed on each other. Their clothing lay in a pile on a blanket within reach of the brush. Now on all fours, he moved onto the clothing separating out Marcie's bra and bikini panties. After fondling them for several moments, the intruder was startled by Marcie's laughter and splashing, compelling him to drop the underwear and retreat stealthily back into the brush.

"Not like this, Jake. Not here in the water," she pleaded.

"Are you afraid the fish will watch us?'

"Come on, silly. Let's go back to the blanket."

As their lake water foreplay had taken Jake to near sexual peak, it was just as well that they moved on shore.

Jake would have prematurely ejaculated and wasted the potion he had for Marcie on the fish. Their bodies appeared wanly, even luminous in the moon's light. Jake first tossed Marcie onto the wild grass and then pulled her onto the blanket. All over her like a ravenous dog on raw hamburger, he kissed both sides of her face and then her mouth. From the watcher's vantage point, the two bodies were still visible, writhing and moaning perhaps no more than a minute. Jake then let out an audible groan and rolled off of Marcie into the cool grass.

Marcie suddenly sat upright and placed her hands cross-ways over her breasts. "What was that? Did you hear something?"

Jake, spent and motionless, spread open like a snow angel, answered with an unintelligible grunt. He hadn't heard anything except his pounding heart.

Marcie grabbed her bra and panties and threw them on quickly. The shorts and halter top followed. "Let's get out of here, Jake. I'm spooked."

"They ain't nobody out here, Marcie. You probably heard a rabbit or possum. " Jake grabbed his briefs and pulled them on with a jerk as though he had gotten what he came for and was now bored with it all. From his cargo pocket he took out the Marlboros, shoving one in his mouth. With a flick of his wrist he popped open the lighter, the one with the Marine seal his father had given him, and struck the flint. After expelling a long, satisfying stream of smoke, he said, "Come on. Let's get the hell out of here. You ain't for shit as a lay."

Marcie detested Jake's snotty attitude, not to mention his hurtful slam, and refrained from even looking at him. She welled up and wiped the draining mucous from her nose with the backs of her fingers. She expected more from him than the 'wham, bam.' But then again, she never figured him for the tender 'after sex' guy. Most of all, however, she was angry with herself for losing her virginity to the likes of Jake Thigpen. She could have waited. Waited for someone special. Now, she realized her first time at this was a mistake. A failure. In fact, if anything, it was painful.

Still in tears, she slid onto the passenger's seat of Jake's Camaro. She thought she would be sick. Mostly, it was the combination of stale cigarettes and leaking oil made her nauseous. Funny. She hadn't minded it on the way *to* the lake.

At just before ten, Jake turned the Camaro onto Sydenstricker, the dirt road that dead-ended about three football fields into the St. Clair house. Marcie told him to stop the car and she would walk the rest of the way. She definitely didn't want to chance her father seeing the headlights and hearing Jake's rusted out muffler.

"What, are you ashamed of me? Afraid your old man will kick my ass? Well, I ain't afraid. Go ahead, get out. Go!" He reached over her to pull the door handle. Marcie sat for a moment looking at Jake, contemptuously, not saying a word.

"Go on, I said. I'm sure you'll tell your daddy you were at the movies with Nancy or Becky. Better get your story straight, so as you don't get tripped up." He then pushed open the door and Marcie swung out. When she slammed the door, the side mirror, loose from his sideswipe with a utility pole, fell down onto the sheet metal.

Jake threw his shifter in reverse, backed out onto Highway 41 and gunned the Camaro south. The roar of his exhaust soon out of earshot, it was suddenly quiet. Deafeningly quiet. As she began walking down Sydenstricker, she failed to see the black SUV that was parked off the dirt road, hidden in the scrub pines. Marcie St. Clair, now soiled and looking older than her eighteen years, walked slowly, head down, in the direction of the faintly visible porch light on the house at the end of the road. A sudden breeze caught up her thick, beautiful hair that shown more strawberry than red in the silvery light of the summer moon.

Starr sat by the window, adjusting her telescope on its tripod in the direction of the Corona Borealis. Because the moon was now high and bright, the cluster was dimmer than usual. But some stars within other ancient constellations in the mid-northern latitude still shone throughout the night sky with the luster of diamonds. By her side was her Star Finder from which she charted and tracked movement, explored colorful nebulae and discovered new bodies of light.

At eleven-thirty, after the local news, Blake turned off the Magnavox and performed a brief radio check with Linc who sat in his patrol car outside of the Oasis. Sooner or later inebriated patrons would exit the bar, climb under the wheel and start their cars. That's when Linc would nab them.

"Starr, are you in bed yet."

"I'm scanning the Northern Cross, Daddy. A few more minutes okay?"

Blake poured himself a half glass of cold milk and stepped out on the front porch for a breath of fresh air. His presence immediately interrupted the chorus of tree frogs, and all that remained audible was the whining of car tires out on 41 a mile or so away. The night air was less humid than usual, evermore evident by the clarity of the full moon now twelve o'clock high. After downing the last gulp of the velvet nectar, he turned to go back inside. At that moment, Rupert Kolb's Suburban slowed in front of the house to turn into the driveway next door. Blake stood a moment with the door open for no particular reason, staring in the direction of his neighbor's house.

Starr, who had already turned out her light and was placing the lens cap on her telescope, heard Kolb's tires on the gravel. She looked down just in time to see his headlights go out.

Kolb exited his vehicle and glanced back in Blake's direction. Their eyes locked for a moment, but neither acknowledged the other. Kolb then turned his back, manually opened his garage door and disappeared from view. Blake heard the door travel down its rollers and then slam shut.

The luminous red numbers on the clock radio read three forty-two when Blake was jolted awake by the phone on the night stand. He fumbled the receiver a couple of times then brought it to his ear. "Hello," he grunted.

"Blake," the voice said. "Charlie St.Clair here."

Blake cleared his throat to get his voice. "Yeah, Coach. What's going on?" He glanced back at the clock. "It's almost four. Is everything all right?"

"I don't know, Blake. Marcie didn't come home last night. She was supposed to be out with some girls and home by eleven. I called Nancy Earle, who Marcie said she'd be goin' to the movies with, but Nancy after lyin' to me and her parents, admitted she was coverin' for Marcie. Said Marcie was out with that Thigpen creep. I'm afraid she's over there in that trailer camp."

Blake sat up and twisted the knob on the lamp. "Well, Coach, if that's the case, what do you want me to do?"

"I want you to go over there and bring her home, Blake. If *I* go, I'm liable to end up killin' that boy."

"Coach, I'd think if she stayed over with him, his mom would know it. That woman may be a little rough around the edges, but she wouldn't allow that to happen." Blake then swung his bare legs off the bed and stood.

"Do me this favor, son. Please."

"Okay, Coach. If it'll make you feel better, I'll *go* out there and talk with Mrs. Thigpen. I hope to God Marcie's there or with some other friend. But I wouldn't worry about it. I'm sure there's an explanation for it all."

St. Clair paused and sighed. "Thanks, Blake. I owe ya. Marcie's mom is right upset, you know."

Actually, Blake *was* worried. He knew Marcie would

never stay out and risk the ire of her father, unless the Thigpen boy had gotten her drunk or popped an Ecstasy in her drink. Marcie was a little wild and fun-loving, but she was a good girl and otherwise responsible.

Blake went to Starr's room to check on her, then left and locked the front door behind him. If he stayed out well into the morning, he would later call Mrs. Baker and have her go by to check on Starr. Mrs. Baker kept a key to the Ravenel house in a candy dish by the front door.

The trailer park without a name was off 601 between the Grange Hall and the South Georgia Flea Market. Blake wasn't quite sure which metal box belonged to the Thigpens, but it didn't take him long to spot Jake's faded blue Camaro. Alongside the Camaro sat a rusted-out, hoodless '62 Chevy on blocks. It all reminded Blake of something his cousin, Lawrence, said after returning from a Georgia-Auburn game. "Yeah, Blake. Just came back from Alabama. You know, the state where all the cars are up on blocks and the *houses* are on wheels."

He cut the lights on the Blazer and picked up his mike.

"Linc, this is Blake. Radio check. Come in. Over."

After a few moments Linc's slightly garbled voice came through the speaker. "Chief. What are you doin' up at this hour? I didn't expect to hear from you till after seven."

"Marcie St. Clair is missing. She didn't come home from an apparent date with Jake Thigpen."

"Jake Thigpen! That little rat? What's she doin' messin'

with the likes of him?" Linc paused and then keyed back in. "Over," he added.

"I don't know, Linc," Blake responded with a sigh. "Something isn't right about this. I'm at the Thigpens now, getting ready to go in. Over."

"Do you need backup?"

"No, no. No reason for that. It's just Mrs. Thigpen and Jake."

"Okay. Standin' by, over."

"Ravenel, out."

Blake grabbed his foot long flashlight and exited the Blazer. After stepping up onto the cinderblock steps, he knocked lightly on the side of the mobile home. He could hear stumbling around inside and felt the trailer vibrate from foot steps. A woman's smoky voice called from inside. "Who the hell's out there and what do you want?!"

"Mrs. Thigpen, it's Chief of Police Ravenel. Would you open up, please?"

The light on the side of the trailer came on and a collection of flying bugs immediately began flapping around it. After the door swung open about halfway, the forty-five year old face of Wanda Thigpen came into view. Her eyes were puffy from perhaps one too many cigarettes and huge rollers containing her bleached-blonde hair lay all over her head. The flimsy housecoat did little to hide the two hundred pounds that bulged beneath it. And then her bridge was missing. She was hard to look at.

"Chief, what the hell's goin' on? Is somebody daid?"

"Why would you ask that Mrs. Thigpen?"

"No reason, I guess. At this ungodly hour somebody *better* be daid or tell me I'm a Sweepstakes winner."

"Mrs. Thigpen, have you seen Marcie St. Clair? She wouldn't be in here with Jake, would she?"

"Marcie who?" the woman asked. "You're not talkin' about that football coach's girl, are you?"

"Yes I am."

"Ain't nobody here except me and Jake. Why the hell would she be with Jake? She's a whole different class than us. Not to say we're any kind of trash, mind you."

"No ma'am. We have reason to believe Jake and Marcie were out on a date tonight."

She gave him a puzzled look. "Jake was out earlier, but it damn sure weren't with that St. Clair girl."

"Would you please wake him, ma'am?"

Wanda stood in the doorway a few seconds, then said, "Oh, all right. Come on in here." She then yelled loud enough for lights in other trailers to come on. *"Jake! Get your ass out of bed! The law wants to talk to you!"*

Blake heard Jake's feet hit the floor in his bedroom and soon the boy stood beside his mother in nothing but his checkered boxers.

"Get back in there and put some pants on. Chief don't want to see you half nekkid like this."

Jake returned to the living room, zipping up his cargo pants. "What's goin' on?' he asked, reaching for his smokes.

Blake moved in on him and gestured toward a dining chair. "Sit down, Jake. I have a few questions for you."

The boy obeyed without a word, flicked the lighter and lit up. "Okay. What gives?"

"Jake, now I want you think about how you answer this and it had better be the truth. Were you with Marcie St. Clair tonight?"

Jake swallowed hard and took a quick drag. "Why do you want to know? Did I break some kind of law?"

"I'm just asking you a straight-up question, son. Did you see her tonight?"

"Maybe. Did her old man sic you on me?" Another drag.

Wanda slapped him on the back of the head. "Don't sass the man, Dummy. Now you answer him proper."

"Okay. Yeah. We went out. We went to the lake and I took her home. So what?"

"What time was that?"

Jake settled back in his chair and tapped out his half-smoked cigarette. The trailer must have been 95 degrees inside and sweat rolled down his skinny, bare chest. "Nine-thirty. I don't know, maybe ten.

"You're sure about that, are you? Where exactly did you let her out?"

"On Sydenstricker, just a few feet off 41. She was afraid her ol' man might hear my exhaust. You see, there's a hole in my muffler and since he don't like me....well, you know the rest." He nervously lit up another Marlboro which added insult to the oppressive heat in the metal box.

"That means you let her out three or four hundred yards from the house."

"If you say so." Jake began to fidget. "What's all this about, anyway?"

"She never made it home, Jake." The chief leaned into him.

Jake jumped from his chair to his feet. "What? How could that be? There weren't no other place to go from there *but* home. That's nuts."

"Okay, Jake, you need to tell me everything about last night."

Jake sat back down and placed his hands on his knees. He told Blake that he and Marcie went swimming in Coowatchee, then afterward, made out a little. She got kind of huffy and said to take her home. That's all he knew.

"Did you see her start walking toward home when you let her out?"

"No. I just beat it out of there. I could tell she was pissed off about something and that pissed me off too."

For a good long time Blake stared at the boy who continued sucking on his cigarette every five seconds like clockwork. Finally, he said, "All right, Jake. You'd better be telling me the truth. I guess that's it for now. Better hope she turns up. If you hear from her today, you be sure to let me know."

Jake nodded, but didn't reply.

"Sorry to bother you, Mrs. Thigpen." Blake returned his cap to his head and left. Before he even made it to the Blazer, he heard the yelling and an audible slap. Then another.

It was nearly five, and after checking on Starr and brushing his teeth, Blake radioed Linc to meet him at the St. Clair house at six. As he turned onto Sydenstricker, he drove slowly, scanning the scrub oaks and pines for any signs of foul play. Bessie Cotter's was the first house on the left, standing crookedly, dilapidated, weatherworn. Bessie was usually on her porch day *and* night enjoying her Copenhagen, brown spit shooting from her toothless mouth like BBs. But five on a Sunday morning, she was either sleeping or getting ready for church. And Bessie did not dip on Sundays.

He passed the Cochran and Binfield houses on the right, half way to the end of the lane. No lights, no stirring in either place. If Marcie did not turn up during the day, Blake would start his canvass with them.

"Come in, fellas." The coach greeted Blake and Linc with the usual vice grip. Standing in the hallway behind him was Beulah St. Clair, eyes red and swollen, handkerchief in hand.

"Morning, Mrs. St. Clair. I know you've had a worrisome night." Blake then turned to Coach. "I just left Wanda Thigpen's place. Jake *was* with Marcie last night…."

"Damn! Damn!" Coach interrupted, banging the side of his fist on the hall wall. "Was she there? Does he know where she is?"

"No on both questions, Coach. He says he dropped her off on the upper end of the road at the 41 intersection so you wouldn't hear his car. Guess he was afraid you'd start something up with him."

"Damn straight I would've. I'da probably killed the boy."

"I don't mind telling you, Charlie, I'm a little concerned myself. And I can't begin to imagine what's going through your mind. We'll get up with all her friends and if she didn't spend the night with any of them, I'll notify Sheriff Harper and the GBI. Then I'll put together a search team. We'll begin at your house and work backwards toward 41." Blake looked again at Beulah who had begun sobbing. He leaned into Coach and added softly, "We'll check the lake too, Charlie."

St. Clair put his hand on Blake's shoulder. "You fellas do what you need to do to find her." He began to well up. It was the first time Blake had ever seen the tender side of the iron man.

The coach then turned to Linc, grabbing his over-sized bicep. "Linc, my man. I was barely older than this boy here when I took over the football program at Pine River. Your chief here was a natural, mind you. The best leader and best arm I ever saw play the game. He won me my first championship, you know. Then there was Bobby Zale a couple of years later. We had some great teams…"

Linc knew the coach was just rattling on, trying to take both his and Beulah's mind off the moment. "I know, Coach. I was there for all them games. My boy played for you too, you know."

"Yep, I remember James. He was some hitter all right. When he nailed 'em, they didn't get up."

Linc held out his hand and it was like two bear paws joining. "We'll find her, Coach. Don't you and the Misres worry. We won't do anything else today till we do."

It was five minutes past eight. Bobby was now on duty and Linc refused to go home. The three of them went to the Kudzu for coffee and strategy. The St. Clairs had given Blake a list of Marcie's friends and each of the officers would split it up and question four or five best friends to see if Marcie had spent the night with any of them.

Bobby rocked his chair back and balanced it on two legs. "Maybe we need to bring the Thigpen boy in and pound on him a little. Without Big Mama protecting him, he might just sing a different tune."

Blake took a gulp of his coffee and winced as the hot liquid burned his throat. "Well, if we do believe what the boy says, there was no way for Marcie to get from the road where she was let out to any of her friends without walking or driving three or four miles. Both St. Clair cars were still in the driveway this morning, so she didn't drive anywhere. Bobby, you and I will go speak to the girls, and Linc, go check with the people out on Sydenstricker to see if they saw her. Maybe they heard something. We'll meet back at the station at noon. If she still hasn't materialized, I'll call Sheriff Harper to bring over some deputies. Then we'll get them and some of the fellows together to search the woods around Sydenstricker."

"I still say Jake Thigpen knows more than he told you," said Bobby. "A little one on one and *I'll* get it out of him."

Blake ignored the comment, dropped a couple of bucks on the table and stood. "Let's get to it, guys."

As Blake had feared, none of Marcie's friends had seen her since the previous afternoon. Sarah Davis' father told him that he wouldn't put it past that Thigpen boy to have 'done somethin' to her.' Bobby radioed in a negative report as well. "Nobody's seen her, Blake."

At twelve thirty Sheriff Harper and two deputies met the Pine River officers at the town hall. The word had already spread about Marcie's disappearance. Prayers for her well-being were offered up by the pastors of the First Baptist Church and New Life Tabernacle prior to the dismissal of their congregations. The mayor and no less than fifty concerned citizens joined the officers to help search. One of them was Starr.

"Go home, Starr. You're not going out in those woods. I don't want to end up sending someone to look for *you*."

"I may be twelve, Daddy, but I'm just as much a citizen as anyone else in this town."

Blake didn't respond to her. "Bobby, take Starr home on your way out to the St. Clairs".

She cast a defiant look in her dad's direction and turned away abruptly. Blake shook his head. The harsh words between them had certainly become more prevalent in the last few days. He didn't have the time *or* patience to engage in another argument with her. As Starr was trying desperately to become an adult, she demanded respect and credibility from her dad for being older and more mature than her twelve years. What would the next five or six years be like in the Ravenel house?

On the way to the patrol car Bobby put his arm around her. "Listen, Starbright, your Daddy just wants you to be safe, that's all. There could be something bad out there and you could run up on it."

Starr got in and slammed the door forcefully. It was her way of telling Bobby not to patronize her. "So you think I'm a child, too, Bobby Zale. And just to think, I was starting to like you." She squinted her eyes at him menacingly, but with a mischievous smile. "So *do* you?"

"Do I what?"

"Think I'm a child."

He buckled his seat belt and grinned. "Well, let's just say I'll give you a couple of years."

"Till what?"

"Till I ask your old man if I can take you out."

That made her heart jump a couple of extra beats and her face took on a warm glow. The very thought of Bobby the Hunk telling her that, whether he meant it or not, caused her to have to reach for a deep breath. "Can we swing by the church on the way home?"

"Sure. Why?"

"Church ought to be over and I want to catch up to Tommy Lee. He's probably hanging around out front with the group." Actually, she knew Tommy didn't even go to church that day and she just wanted Lydia Shelton and Janie Walls to see her cruising by with Bobby Zale.

And they did. Starr's nose was in the air as the car passed by, but peripherally, she took note of their stares.

CHAPTER SIX

About fifty volunteers and six law officers congregated at the front steps of the large two-story Greek Revival. Coach St. Clair stood on the veranda looking down, thanking the men. They all assured him that Marcie would turn up unharmed. Maybe she just forgot to tell her parents she was spending the night with a girlfriend, that's all.

At two-thirty they split into groups and spread to the four winds. Blake and Linc were to each command a dozen or so men to cover the north quadrant between the house and Highway 41 and into the east woods to Myers Creek. Bobby, Sheriff Harper and deputies took the remainder of the party out about two clicks to the west and south. If someone in a group found something, the controlling officer would fire two shots and report to Blake via radio.

Delbert Kennedy who was pushing his way through

the brush about 150 yards parallel to Sydenstricker, stopped to rest on the trunk of a fallen Live Oak. Having plugged away for over forty five minutes, he was hot, tired and thirsty. He had searched down to 41 and crossed over the highway into Horace Wagner's bean field, then realized he had gone well beyond the established perimeter. Having trudged twenty yards further west, he had finally circled back across the highway back toward the St Clair house, picking his way through a grove of stubborn scrub pines. Delbert sat for more than two minutes, breathing heavily and feeling his fifty-six years in the sweltering South Georgia sun. He sucked in four or five gulps of his canteen water and wiped his bald head with a blue bandana handkerchief. To his right he heard the popping and cracking of twigs and such, catching sight of seventy two year old Fred Zimmerman.

"What're you doin' sittin' down on the job, young feller? Not tuckered out are you?" A huge grin was on his weathered face.

Delbert laughed. "I should be in your shape when I'm old as you, Zimmy." Fred returned the laugh and moved on.

Delbert had only another two hundred yards to go before he was back at Coach's porch. But first he wasted the last of his water and mopped his forehead yet another time. It had to be 95 degrees. A large crow the color of midnight sat perched on a pine branch high above his head, its coat giving off a silken sheen in the merciless sun. After it screamed out a couple of bodacious caws, it swooped down into the thicket between two twenty foot scrub oaks perhaps fifty feet away. Three other crows flapped and scurried when the larger one flew in. Delbert stood up and walked toward the brush, startling the crows and causing all of them to take flight. They made certain to express their anger on their way up to the branches of an adjacent pine.

He curiously peered into the brush, first catching sight of what looked like a mop of dark red hair. As he moved closer in, his horrified eyes fixed on the pale, scantily clad body of a young woman. Sweeping nausea came over him and the vomit came swiftly. Violently. Because of the burning, choking matter in his throat, he was momentarily unable to call out. Marcie St. Clair's beautiful face was now distorted and the color of ashen quartz. Her naked breasts were soaked with the red-brown blood that had spurted from the deep gash on her neck. A cavernous gash that extended from below one ear across the neck to the other.

Somehow through his tears, nausea, and raw throat, he was able to scream, "Fred! Fred! Over here! Get Bobby!"

Within seconds Bobby Zale and the remainder of his team converged on the death scene. Delbert Kennedy was still bent over, hands on knees and retching a second time. A chorus of gasps and groans ensued and Bobby fired the deafening two shots that the remainder of the party and the St. Clairs had dreaded they would hear.

Now, as many as forty volunteers came flocking to the area, Blake among them. He told them all to stay back from the crime scene, taking no chance that any evidence would be disturbed. Moving in carefully, alone, Blake knelt a few feet from the body. He recognized the familiar M.O. immediately. Marcie's arms were crossed just below her breasts and beneath them, the Raggedy Ann in the red and white striped dress. And blood-red hair. The artificial smile on the doll's face seemed to mock the girl cradling it.

Blake heard yelling in the distance, "It's Coach! Let him through!"

Springing from his crouched position, Blake ran toward the trembling man. *"No!"* he exclaimed, intercepting and holding him. "No, Coach. Please stay where you are."

But St. Clair broke loose and made a bee-line to the spot where his daughter lay. Blake's heart sank even deeper as he watched Coach fall onto all fours beside Marcie's body and weep bitterly. Blake bent down and placed his arm around the broken man and pulled him to his feet. "Come on, Charlie. You don't need to see this. I've got to get the GBI team in here. Let's go back to…" But then Blake's tears began as well, and he could not continue. Both men stood embraced for as long as a minute until Bobby began leading them from the scene. When they had taken a few steps, the large leader crow swooped down from the pine to do more pecking on Marcie's body. Blake picked up a smooth stone and hurled it at the bird. When it lit up to a branch about ten feet away from the body, rapacious and poised to dive again, Blake drew his Glock, aimed and fired one deadly shot that disintegrated the bird.

Coach sat down on the same fallen tree where Delbert Kennedy had rested some ten minutes before. His face lay motionless in his hands. Blake stood beside him with his hand on his shoulder. "Charlie, I want you to go back to the house now. Okay? Beulah will need you. I'll come by later to see you. I've got to wait for the GBI."

The coach looked up at Blake, eyes swollen and red. "How could somethin' like this happen, Blake? How could it happen to my Marcie?" He began to sob again. The words would not come for Blake. All he could manage was to grip Coach's shoulder in silent consolation.

"Linc, walk home with him and then I want *you* to go home and get some rest. Bobby," he called, motioning him over with a jerk of his head. When Bobby stepped over, Blake led him out of earshot.

"Go pick up Jake Thigpen," he said lowly.

"You got it, Chief."

Before Linc and Charlie St. Clair left the scene, the coach turned once more to peer through the clump of teasel at his daughter who lay butchered and violated. His faced, racked with pain and horror, he said, "Look after her, Blake. Please, son, get her out of here as soon as they're done."

Blake nodded.

The GBI Crime Scene Unit arrived on the scene at 4:15 and placed the familiar yellow tape around the trees about fifty feet in each direction from the body. Blake dismissed the volunteers who had remained, thanking them for their service. He and Del Kennedy exchanged looks, but no words. The eyes reflected each man's pain and sadness. Blake stood stoic and practically motionless for more than an hour, watching the GBI work the area. They needed to be thorough, but the time they took was agonizing. He just wanted Marcie out of there.

It was almost seven before the coroner arrived to make Marcie's death official. Besides his heartsickness, Blake felt helpless, even responsible in some way. Maybe because it was *his* town and now one of his own was murdered. Somebody close to him. He had seen death many, many times in Vietnam. But that was impersonal and he had become callused over there when it came to death, even when children such as this were killed in the crossfire. It was just as well that he remained at Marcie's death scene these hours. Being with Coach and his wife in this time of their immense grief… that would have killed him.

On the way to the station Blake received a call from Bobby. "He's not here, Blake. His car's gone and his mother hasn't seen him all day."

"Okay. I'll notify Sheriff Harper to put an APB out on him. Stay there and stake out the trailer park for the remainder of the evening. I'll swing through town and look for his car."

By dusk the news of Marcie St. Clair's murder had spread through the community of Pine River like a prairie fire. In the waning daylight a long line of curiosity seekers cruised slowly along 41 with intentions of turning down Sydenstricker. Blake sat at the intersection and waved them on. After dark, the traffic ceased. He turned toward the St. Clair house, but stopped. Blake still could not bring himself to go sit with Charlie and Beulah. Backing out again onto 41, he rationalized that they just needed to be alone at this time. He would see them in the morning.

Blake stopped by Katie's around ten to retrieve Starr. For a few moments they all sat in the living room, somber and silent. He was worried about how Starr was taking this all in as he could see she was visibly shaken. She looked down at her lap much of the time and said nothing. Up until today, she had gone on and on to Tommy Lee and her friends about last weekend's dumpster finding. It was an exciting event, but tragic, she was sure to add. It gave the dull little town of Pine River a much needed shot in the arm. But nobody knew the Scott woman. This time, it was different. The victim was Marcie Rose. And Marcie had baby-sat Starr more than a dozen times.

Blake's eyes remained transfixed on the Norman Rockwell print on Katie's wall over her piano. Life was simple and funny to the artist. Rockwell's paintings told stories without words. They depicted a warmth and innocence much like what Blake knew Pine River to be when he was a child. It was a safe time when doors were not locked and life was carefree in small-town Georgia, seemingly preserved and exemplified by the chiming of church bells, the smell of sweet breads baking at Donnegans, and the cold, crisp Christmas air.

Katie sat beside Blake on the sofa and lightly placed her hand on his knee. "Have you eaten anything?"

"No. Just a granola bar this morning."

She slid forward on the couch and stood. "I'll fix you a sandwich."

"No. No thanks," he replied, grabbing her hand gently. "You wait on people all day long. Anyway, I don't think I could stomach anything." The ever present image of Charlie St. Clair's only child, bloodied, pale and violated, had killed his hunger pangs. And there was that doll lying atop Marcie's stomach. What was that about? Was it some kind of sick, psychopathic symbol?

Blake looked at Starr who remained noticeably and uncharacteristically quiet. He knew she was hurting inside. He would now be extraordinarily vigilant when it came to her. She would stay home and under the eye of Mary Alice Baker every moment of the day, if he had to chain her there.

He moved to his feet and held out his hand. "Come on, Starr. Let's go home," he said softly. She gathered up her sketchpad and took his hand.

On the way home she said nothing. Only her eyes spoke the language of sadness and fear. Blake stroked the back of her neck which prompted her to lean into him and place her small arms around his waist. The tears followed.

After a few moments he performed a radio check with Bobby. Jake Thigpen had still not come home. Blake told him to canvass the town, then return periodically to stake out the trailer park. Sleep would not come right away and if Blake had not been so concerned about leaving Starr alone, he would have swept the town and surrounding area the remainder of the night as well.

When he was certain that Starr was in bed asleep, Blake returned downstairs to his bedroom. The gun belt and shirt came off and he plopped wearily into the chair by his bed. Starr's other sketchpad lay on the night table where he had placed it the night before. When he picked it up, several sheets of paper fell out. They were the blown up microfiche copies of newspaper articles, one of which included the photo of a smiling, seemingly happy family of four. Blake read each of the five daily accounts of the gruesome Morris murders. Where was Stanley Morris now? He compared Starr's sketch of an aged Morris. As much as he hated to admit it, the sketch did resemble his neighbor, Rupert Kolb, a man with whom he had not exchanged words more than three times in as many years. Blake closed the sketchpad and laid it atop his gun belt. He leaned his head back against the cushion of the wingback. "Will check you out tomorrow, Mr. Kolb," he said in his mind.

At 0700, Monday morning, a joint task force consisting of GBI Senior Agent Harmon Nelson, Agent Lanham, FBI Special Agent Jim Puckett from the Savannah office, Sheriff Harper and the officers of Pine River met at the police station. Anna Mae busied herself by bustling from coffee pot to lawman, handing out cups of her kerosene cocktail. Blake was amused watching each of them wince as they took their first sips.

Marcie St. Clair's death scene photos had been developed overnight by the GBI crime lab and were added to the mobile board containing a myriad of crime scene photos from the other three murders.

"Definitely the same killer, Chief," said Nelson. "Actually all the dolls have borne the same label, *Darling Dolls*, made in Akron, Ohio. Trouble is, you can buy these dolls most anywhere. We've previously checked all the doll and toy stores in the Savannah area and there haven't been any *bulk* doll sales. Of course, the killer could have bought them one at a time or even from different stores. The Raggedy Ann is a popular little doll."

"Yeah. Even my daughter, Starr, has one of these that her mother got for her when she was a baby. By the way, did you happen by the store here in Pine River? *Roy's Toys*. Run by an old classmate of mine, Roy McIntyre."

"No. Didn't know you had a toy store here. I'll check it out today," Nelson replied.

"I'll take you there myself, if I'm not stepping on you guys' toes."

"You're the law here, Blake. No problem on my end. How about you, Jim?"

Puckett nodded. "As long as you keep us informed of any findings on this or the Scott case, Chief."

"Fine," said Blake. "Now, wonder if you fellows can do me a favor? Run a background through your systems on a man named Rupert Kolb, supposedly from

New Jersey. Somewhere around here is his old Jersey tag number."

"Why do you ask, Blake?" asked Lanham. "Do you suspect his connection to these murders?"

"He lives next door to me. Moved here two or three years ago. He waited almost a year before getting his Georgia tag and I had to say something to him about it. I don't really have any real reason to tie him into the murders. He's just a strange dude, that's all."

"I'll run the man," offered Puckett. "Should have something by late afternoon."

At 11:30, Blake and Agent Nelson went by the Kudzu for a sandwich. Katie took a short break and stopped to talk to Blake by the vintage jukebox when he came out of the restroom.

"God, Blake," she said. "I've never seen people so scared in this town. Mabel Patterson at the beauty parlor was in here a few minutes ago and said she's already made three appointments for hair color changes. Bunky Carver, whose two daughters both have copper red hair, wants to make brunettes out of them. And Jane Tolliver, who's every bit seventy-five and has been tinting her hair Lucy Ball red for twenty years, wants to go back to gray. You should hear all the talk in here."

"I know. We're going to have a real chore keeping the lid on this town. The mayor is calling a special meeting with us and the town counsel for tomorrow evening. It'll be quite a spell before this dies down. It will also put a real damper on Rebels football this fall."

Katie smiled and leaned her forehead into Blake's. "You guys. Does everything in the world have to center around football?"

He smiled back. Her little quip was just what he needed at that moment. But it was the *coach* he had on his mind when he said that. His heart ached for the man.

Nelson, still sitting at the counter, took note of the quick kiss Katie stole from Blake. He winked as Blake returned to his stool. "Pretty gal. Your wife?"

"No no. Just a friend I've known for a bunch of years."

"And very well, I take it." He slapped Blake on the back. "*I* should have that kind of friend." Nelson leaned back down to his BLT.

About two-fifteen Blake and Nelson pulled into the parking lot behind Roy's Toys. "This could be ugly," Blake said, throwing the gearshift into park.

"Why's that?"

Blake unsnapped his seat belt and positioned the ball cap on his head. "You'll see. I doubt we've said a dozen words to one another in ten years."

"Bad blood?"

"Something like that."

The bell at the top of the door made the familiar jingle, prompting Roy McIntyre to look up from behind the cash register. Staring at the men and showing no emotion, Roy watched them move throughout the store perusing the merchandise. High wall shelves on either side contained mostly boxed items such as model cars, planes and Breyer horses. Four rows of standing shelves in the middle of the room had the usual inventory of a K Mart or Toys R Us. But through the years Roy's store had been known for its sets of miniatures such as meticulously-painted soldiers of Napoleon's or Robert E. Lee's armies. And then one complete row of shelves contained boxed dolls of every sort, including the popular Chatty Cathies and the new craze, the Cabbage Patch doll that came complete with its own name and a date of birth. Every kind of doll except the Raggedy Ann.

Roy was no longer the lean and handsome blonde 'boy next door' that he was a dozen years before. The hair was gone, fifty pounds had been added, and his winning smile had been replaced long ago by a semi-permanent scowl. And the latter did not set well with parents who preferred that their toddlers be addressed by a friendlier face.

Roy had openly avoided Blake through the years, but when they did cross paths, he offered only a glare and a nod. There *had* been one verbal altercation. Blake remembered only that it was something involving a delivery truck impeding traffic in front of the store. But it wasn't really about the truck. It was about history. It was about Roy's sour grapes and vehement disdain over Blake marrying Luann. Even though Blake had once attempted to rekindle their old high school friendship by inviting him on a fishing trip down the Intercoastal, Roy snubbed him. For nearly fourteen years he had remained distant and non-conversive.

Blake approached the counter and the two men glared at one other.

"Roy."

"Chief."

They stood for a moment saying nothing, holding their stares. Then it was Roy who broke the ice. "What brings you here, Blake? And who the hell is the suit?"

Blake jerked his head in the agent's direction. "This is Harmon Nelson, Georgia Bureau of Investigation, Roy. *You* know what's happened in this town over the past few days, especially yesterday. We're here to ask you something."

"Ask me what?" he replied, shortly.

"Have you had any recent sales of the Raggedy Ann doll or remember who may have purchased more than one over the past couple of years?"

"How the hell should I remember *who* bought *what* in here. People come in and out all day long. A lot of them buy dolls."

"I'm just specifically asking about the Raggedy Ann, Roy. Surely you haven't moved a lot of these, considering all these new walking, talking dolls."

"Okay. Maybe I remember selling a few last Christmas, but none since then."

"You're sure."

"Hell, yes I'm sure." Roy fired, revealing a surging agitation.

"Would you mind going over your old invoices from the last six months or so? Maybe Mindy sold one or two while you were out."

"Yeah, I *do* mind. It would take me hours to check every sales receipt since Christmas."

Blake's glare became more intense. He then shifted his foot and looked down at a loose board in the ancient wooden floor. "Better fix that before someone falls."

"Did you come here to lecture me about risk?"

Blake looked up and fired a laser. "Marcie St. Clair is dead, Roy. One of this town's children has been murdered. A doll that could have come from your store was found on her body. I wish *she* had those same hours of life that you think are so *inconvenient*."

Roy's face advertised his embarrassment like a pink neon sign. "Okay," he said in resignation. "I got probably three boxes of receipts back in my office. If you want to go through that shit, be my guest." Obviously, it wasn't complete resignation.

"Maybe some other day. Just don't let them get lost."

When the officers reached the Blazer, Nelson stopped Blake short, hand on arm. "What the hell was all that about? Not only was that *apathy* at its worst, he acted like he was trying to actually impede this investigation. And, obviously you and this guy ain't bosom buddies. What gives?"

"Long story, Harmon. Maybe another day."

When Blake returned to the station, Harper had departed, but Puckett and Lanham were still there flipping through flyers and mug pages of known child molesters, rapists and other sex offenders. Most of the vermin in the photos didn't fit the profile of a serial killer of young women. Unfortunately, or perhaps just the opposite, fortunately, there was no such collection of mug shots of serial killers. But this killer could be anyone. And even though he may not fit the mold of the faces in the books, he was still a sexual predator. He had either raped or had consensual sex with his victims before killing them. And he had left his prey either partially or fully nude. What continued to baffle them was the rag doll. What did it represent?

"How's it going, fellows?"

Lanham mashed a half-smoked cigarette into an ash tray. "I think we're wasting our time goin' through these, Blake. The killer could be in here, but none of us think so. Most of these are just perverts."

"They're *all* perverts, Mr. Lanham," added Linc. "But you're right about the killer not bein' in any of these mug shots. They're pedophiles and sex fiends. And the rapists are just that…rapists. This dude, though, he's somethin' different. He's straight out of that movie, *Psycho*."

"That may be," agreed Puckett. "But Norman Bates was just a psychopathic killer with mother issues. Our killer is a hunter. Cold and calculated."

Blake nodded. "What do you think, Bobby? You haven't said much."

"Well, obviously the killer has an agenda. What, we don't know. But I suspect our man is smart. He leaves only his calling card…the doll. No other clues. No fibers or hairs. No evidence. He's good."

"No, Bobby," replied Blake. "No one's ever that good. He *will* slip up. And it's likely to be the most trivial thing that will hang him. Oh, he thinks he's smart, all right. But he *will* make that mistake."

Agent Puckett began stuffing his briefcase, preparing to leave. "Your man, Kolb. We're going to need more information on him, Chief. The New Jersey tag belonged to a female named Bonnie Wagner from Tinton Falls, now deceased. The car was never reported stolen and it's possible before the woman died, she sold or transferred the car to Kolb. But there's no record of any Rupert Kolb in New Jersey over the past ten years of records."

Blake leaned back in his chair and locked his fingers behind his head. "My mystery man neighbor is getting stranger by the moment. I'll take it from here. Thanks."

"Let me know. I'll keep digging, otherwise."

As Blake was on his way home, Sheriff Harper called him. "Just to let you know, the State Troopers pulled over your suspect, Thigpen. He's sittin' in my jail right now. Your jurisdiction. Do you want him?"

"You bet. I'll send Bobby Zale to pick him up." Blake then double keyed his mike. "Bobby, are you back out at the trailer camp?"

"Yep, just pulled in."

"Go by county lock-up and get Jake Thigpen. Harper has him."

"Would be my pleasure, Chief."

"In one piece, Bobby. No rough stuff."

There was a pause on the other end that made it evident Bobby was looking forward to do a little head-knocking. "Roger that, Chief."

Jake Thigpen sat handcuffed in a chair next to Blake's desk with Bobby standing behind him like a bar bouncer, arms folded on his chest. Blake was behind the desk reading the coroner's report on Marcie St. Clair. He hadn't even acknowledged Jake when Bobby sat him down. Finally Blake looked up and cast a cold, pedant stare at the boy.

"Has he been Mirandized, Bobby?"

"He has. I read him his rights at county."

"Good. You understand those rights, Jake?"

"Yes, sir."

"Do you want an attorney here?"

"I can't afford no attorney. Anyway, why would I need one? I ain't done nothin' wrong."

Blake rose from his chair and sat on the edge of his desk, arms crossed as usual. "You admitted to me yesterday morning you were with Marcie the night before. You said you made out a little. What does 'making out' mean to you, Jake?"

The boy swallowed hard, causing his Adam's apple to slide up and down. "Well, you know. Kissin' and feelin' her up some."

"Jake, I have a nurse from the clinic coming over here in a few minutes to draw blood from you."

"For what?"

"For lab purposes, son. Will you voluntarily submit to that or do I need to get a court order from Judge Monahan?"

"I got nothin' to hide. Suck it *all* out if you want?"

Bobby slapped the back of Jake's head, rattling the boy's teeth.

"Ow, man," he yelped, wincing and jumping to his feet. "What the hell's *your* problem?"

Blake frowned and shook his head at Bobby.

"Sit down, Jake." Blake pointed to the chair. He paused to give his next question some effect. "What if I told you Marcie was raped?"

Jake swallowed again. The eyes were wide and fearful. "I...I didn't rape her, sir."

"The medical examiner found semen in her and there were vaginal tears."

"I wouldn't know about that."

"Jake, if you had sex with Marcie, tell me now. If semen is matched to you, you will be charged with her rape and murder."

Jake jumped up again and Bobby immediately sat him back down hard. The boy looked as if he were going to cry. "I didn't kill Marcie!" Another swallow. "Okay, okay. We had sex on the lake bank. She wanted to. I didn't force her. And....I think maybe it was her first time. She acted hurt and got mad at me later..."

Bobby interrupted. "Then she got *you* so mad, you killed her, Right, Jake?"

"No!" He yelled back. Then after a pause, asked, "Can I have a cigarette?"

"Neither of us smokes. Finish your story, Jake," said Blake.

"I admit the night didn't end like I wanted. After we....you know, she thought she heard something behind us in the bushes and started puttin' on her clothes. I think she just wanted to go home. She beat it to the car and then just sat there. Demanded I take her home."

Bobby jumped in. "And did you take her directly home?"

"Yeah. Well, no. Just to the beginnin' of her road."

"You just let her out and didn't take her all the way home?"

"Look. She just got pissed about somethin' and wanted out of the car. Mr. Ravenel, I told you that the other night. She didn't want her old man to find out about me and wanted to walk the rest of the way. That's the God's truth. The last time I saw her, she was standin' by my car and that's when I peeled out. God can strike me dead right here if I'm lyin'."

Blake and Bobby exchanged looks. No one said a word for several moments.

Finally, Blake stood and gestured to Bobby to get Jake to his feet. "All right, son. We're going to fingerprint you now and then wait for the nurse."

"Then you'll let me go?"

"Jake, I think we have enough circumstantial evidence to hold you. You'll be here at least until the coroner's inquest at which time we'll put this in the D.A.'s hands."

Jake looked away and shook his head. "I didn't kill Marcie, Chief Ravenel," he said softly.

After the fingerprinting, Bobby put Jake in a holding room to wait for the nurse. The elderly Liddy Baines arrived with her medical kit about six-thirty. After placing the rubber tourniquet on Jake's left bicep and swabbing the bend of his arm with an alcohol swatch, she pushed the needle into his vein.

Suddenly, the door to the station house swung open and Charlie St. Clair's bellowing was heard. "Blake, are you back there? Where is that little Jake bastard?"

Bobby ran toward the squad room and was about to reach for the doorknob, when the Coach barreled through, causing the door to strike him in the chest. Like one of his own running backs, the forty-seven year old man sidestepped Bobby, bowled Libby over and sprang onto Jake. The force of his body drove the needle deeper into Jake's arm, causing the boy to scream out in pain. The bright red blood now poured profusely from his arm.

Blake slipped behind the coach and locked his right forearm around his neck. Planting a choke hold he learned in Ranger training, he momentarily cut off the blood flow at the carotid and slowly eased the coach to the floor. He then checked Libby who was dazed, but otherwise fine, then reapplied the tourniquet to Jake's arm. Blake carefully pulled the needle out and applied pressure to the wound with a Kleenex.

Bobby, rather dazed himself, went to the coach's aid and helped him to his feet. "God, Blake. You could have broken Coach's neck over that snivelin' little prick."

"He's okay. Let's get him to the chair. Libby, are you all right?"

She sat on the floor with her back to a desk and hugged her knees. "I reckon so. Well. *That* was a good bit of excitement."

Blake took St. Clair back to his office and placed a coffee cup in his hand filled with cold water. "Coach, it is only because I know your heart is shattered over Marcie that I do not throw you in one of those cells back there. It is also my utmost respect and love for you that I don't suggest to Jake Thigpen that he press assault charges."

The coach gulped down the water and massaged his neck. With a raspy voice he said, "You're still a tough guy, Blake. I'll give ya that. Maybe you'da made an even better rassler than a quarterback."

Blake placed a firm hand on his mentor's shoulder. "Go home, Coach. Let me take care of business here. That's my job. Yours is to be with Beulah. I'll check on you tomorrow."

The pained expression came back into St. Clair's face again and he began to sob a little. Pulling a handkerchief from his pocket, he replied, "It's just hard, Blake. The hardest thing I've had to cope with all my life. Don't know how I can go on, now. And I'll never be able to pick back up this fall."

"You will, Coach. It's easy for me to say that now, but time will take care of this. It will get just a little easier each day."

Wiping his eyes, Coach asked, "When do you think we'll get Marcie back from the coroner?"

"I'd say a couple of days, after he's done his work."

"God, I hate the thoughts of her bein' cut open." He paused and stared blankly at the wall. "Just wanted to know when I can make the funeral arrangements."

"I know. Go on, now. I can drive you and have Bobby bring your car."

"No, I'll be all right." He stood slowly and shook Blake's hand. His grip was not as firm as usual. "Thanks."

Blake accompanied him to the door. St. Clair walked out of the office and passed the wounded Jake. He didn't look his way. Blake watched, sadly, as the coach lumbered pitifully through the front door and into the sultry night air.

CHAPTER SEVEN

On Tuesday morning, Dr. Ben Schwartz from County General went by the station to give Jake a physical. He checked every inch of the boy's body for marks and bruises, finding only fingernail scratches on his back. Were they put there in the heat of passion or to fend off a rapist?

The County Medical Examiner released Marcie's body on Wednesday to Taylor Brothers and the funeral was set for Friday. Blake checked on the coach and Mrs. St. Clair each day, promising that he and the GBI would overturn every stone of evidence to bring their daughter's killer to justice.

On Thursday the lab report was sent to the GBI who in turn placed all evidence in the hands of their forensic scientists. Blake would be informed as soon as practical whether there was strong enough evidence to formally charge Jake Thigpen. Whatever the results, Blake was actually buying Jake's story. The ingredients of fear and remorse were in the boy's voice, but there was sincerity as well. And although Jake may have been a lout, Blake did not believe he was capable of murder. For several reasons. First of all, Jake would have been only fifteen when the Savannah murders were committed. A kid did not commit those murders. The neck wounds on all the victims were made with the same knife and no such blade was found at his trailer home or in his car. There was no evidence of a struggle or foul play in Jake's car nor were there any scratch marks anywhere else on his body other than his back. If Jake were the killer rapist, Marcie would have lacerated his face and neck, not his back. Ben Schwartz had agreed that the back scratches were likely put there in passion.

And Jake just didn't fit the profile of a serial killer. Bobby was right. The murderer was smart. Cunning smart. Jake was neither smart *nor* cunning. Unfortunately for Jake, however, he was apparently the last person to see Marcie St. Clair alive and that made him the only game in town.

On Friday morning just before nine, Blake stood on his front porch with one foot propped upon the banister, a coffee mug in his hand and watching a mother robin pecking at the wet ground to draw out earthworms. She managed to gather three and fly them to a moss-covered branch some thirty feet up where her chicks waited with mouths agape. He could not help but think that this mother bird had built her nest far away from danger, doing all she could to protect her young ones. Yet another even more precious young one who had left the loving protection of a nest that had been made for her now lay in her coffin at Taylor Brothers, having fallen victim to a cruel and dangerous world.

Blake took another sip of his coffee, then noticed the mysterious Mr. Kolb taking a handful of letters down the sidewalk to his mailbox. Who was this man? What was he doing with Bonnie Wagner's car? Why was there no record of a Rupert Kolb in all of New Jersey? Was it mere coincidence that the rag doll murders began when he moved into the area? He wasn't quite old enough for social security and did not leave the house for work. What did he do? And what's with the gimpy leg that makes him drag that one foot? No wonder Starr had her suspicions. After the funeral Blake would call up Agent Puckett again. Was there enough substance in the news articles, the photo and the age-enhanced sketch drawn by a child to get Jim Puckett interested enough to follow up with the Jersey authorities on their cold case?

Starr had made toaster waffles for their breakfast, but neither she nor her dad brought an appetite to the table. As they had been to Marcie's wake the evening prior, they each sat quietly remembering the sweetness of her face, the laughing eyes and Valley Girl expressions. She was 'like, you know, cool beans,' as Starr would say. Blake joined his fingertips at the bridge of his nose and found that a smile had broken out. Then it went away as quickly as it had appeared when the picture of a stone cold face in an open coffin invaded his brain. The mortician had done remarkable work, but Starr had commented that Marcie looked artificial. Like a fake Marcie. Like a face she had seen in a wax museum in Myrtle Beach the summer before. Beulah St. Clair had given the undertaker a high collar dress to hide the nasty gash on Marcie's neck where she had been nearly decapitated. Yet curious viewers passing by the casket tried their best, like tabloid sensationalists, to see any such evidence of the horrible death cut below her chin.

Starr then interrupted their silence. "Remember when she stayed with me last October when you were at that convention in Jacksonville?"

"Yeah, I remember."

"She brought over a bunch of her records and we stayed up all night dancing and eating pizza. I didn't ever tell you, 'cause I thought you'd be mad, but she made me up with lipstick, rouge and eye shadow. We walked down Main Street and I tell you no lie, nobody knew who I was. She told some guys I was her sixteen year old cousin from Atlanta. We laughed all the way home…" Starr then dropped her face in her hands and began to sob.

Blake reached across the table and took the moist hands down and caressed them with his.

"It's not fair, Daddy," she cried. "She never did anything to anyone. She just liked having fun, that's all."

"I know it's not fair, Starbright." He noticed her hands

were limp and shaking, prompting him to squeeze them tighter. "Go ahead and let it out."

"I loved Marcie Rose." She was now blubbering and a glossy film of saliva formed between her lips. She was breaking her father's heart.

"Starr," he began softly. "After the funeral if you'd like to talk to Katie, I think that would be a good thing." Katie was as close to a mother that Starr had, considering Tommy had been like her brother over the years.

Starr nodded and wiped her eyes and nose with a napkin.

"And…now more than ever, I want you to stay in the house for a while. No biking all over town. Are we agreed?'

"Even if Tommy is with me?"

"Even so. I want to know where you are every moment. Okay?"

She snuffed twice and then replied quietly, "Okay." This was not the time to get into one of their debates. Anyway, she definitely didn't feel like going out anywhere.

On normal duty days Blake wore the traditional tan shirt, starched and pleated, military green trousers and a ball cap that boasted the town seal. Today he was in dress blues over which was snapped the Sam Black, a uniform he wore on Founders Day or at the Fourth of July parade. But this day was not to be a day of festivity and gaiety. Today a pall hung over Pine River like a blanketing fog. The town was burying Charlie "the Saint" St. Clair's daughter. Pine River's daughter.

After the funeral and gravesite service, Blake true to his mental vow, called Special Agent Puckett, filled him in on the Trenton newspaper articles and Starr's sleuthing, which he addressed rather sheepishly, then faxed the material to him. Puckett said he would send them on to the Trenton FBI unit.

Trenton advised within twenty minutes that the case on Stanley Morris was officially closed some ten years before. However, New Jersey State Police Captain Bill Bannister who had investigated the grisly Morris family murder as a young detective had kept it alive in his mind. Upon the FBI's call, Bannister was delighted that perhaps there was yet another lead out there and was anxious to talk with Pine River, Georgia's Blake Ravenel.

Saturday afternoon Blake sat in his office reviewing the two incident reports completed by Linc on the burglaries that occurred on simultaneous nights at the Red Dot and the Piggly Wiggly. All that appeared to have been taken were cases of beer and liquor. The perps had spray-painted the surveillance cameras and wore gloves, eliminating all tangible evidence. If it were kids who broke in, they were obviously very smart and careful, having planned the capers well. But, if there was a sudden influx in drunken binges within the teenage community, maybe they were not so smart after all. All ears would be to the ground over the next several weeks. Somebody was going to have a hell of a party and the Pine River force would make it their business to find out who.

The phone rang and it was Lanham at the GBI. The semen found in Marcie was indeed Jake Thigpen's. There was also a small amount of flesh under her nails and that was Jake's as well. Blake had surmised as much already. But that didn't make the boy a killer. However, even though no knife or bloody clothes were to be found in Jake's car or his trailer, the bodily evidence and the fact that he was Marcie's last companion would be enough for the D.A. to indict him. The D.A.'s problem would be the other three murders. There was no way to put Jake at the scene of the Savannah bodies. Anyway, one was committed in Savannah on a night Jake was in the hospital with appendicitis and the second, when he was at the junior prom the year before. If the D.A. asserted that Jake killed Marcie in a fit of rage and placed the doll on her body, where would he have gotten the rag doll so quickly unless Jake planned it as a copy-cat murder? And where was the motive for such pre-meditation? As Blake was sure Jake Thigpen did not kill Marcie St. Clair, he would go to as great a length to prove it as he would be bent on catching the real killer.

The Special of the Day at the Kudzu was Chicken Fried Steak with milk gravy, fried okra and sweet silver corn on the cob, a meal that Blake seldom missed. This was the one day neither he nor Starr would cook. At a quarter till five, the two of them plopped themselves on the vinyl red and chrome bar stools at the counter. Katie brought their water and Blake a cup of coffee, then playfully remarked, "I suppose you want the usual, liver and onions, beets and cauliflower?"

"Yuk!" exclaimed Starr. "*You* know what we want, Katie."

"Yeah," added her dad. "Bring Starr a healthy portion of that liver. Me? I can't eat anything that used to be a filter. You can bring me the steak and gravy."

"Daddy!" Starr chided.

While father and daughter continued to banter, another, larger figure slid onto the stool at Blake's right. Feeling the man's presence at his elbow, Blake found the mayor, Tom McCown.

"Evening, Blake." They shook hands. The mayor had large, meaty hands, but no grip. Blake always wondered how a politician could ever make a successful run with a handshake that felt like he laid a cold dead fish in someone's hand.

Tom, although well-dressed and seemingly a man of culture, tried rather vainly at being a dash in his seersucker suit and red bow tie. With his rotund face and white beard he could have won the Ernest Hemingway look-a-like contest in Key West, hands down. "Katie, sweetheart. I'll take some coffee and give me the special also; but instead of the corn, how about some of those Arsh Taters?" Generally a well-spoken man, this was also a sardonic attempt at red-neckese.

"Some what?" She knew what he meant, but as the mayor went out of his way to command attention when he spoke, she intended to push his buttons a little by making light of his Southern-fried lingo.

"I think he means to say Irish Potatoes, Katie, "Starr said, pleased to serve as his interpreter.

"There, see? That little thing can understand me. You have to put on your Southern ears, Katie girl."

Starr rolled her eyes at Katie.

"What's the deal, Tom?" quizzed Blake. "Thought you'd be entertaining like usual on a Friday night, whipping up one of your gourmet meals." McCown often thought of himself as a Renaissance man, a collector of artifacts and paintings, and a man who loved to entertain by preparing epicurean delights for his select group of friends.

The mayor didn't answer. His jocular expression suddenly changed like an ill wind and his face drew up into a pompous scowl. He took a deep breath and let it out, forcefully. "I don't have to tell you, Blake, how revered Coach is in this town. Hell, I know you're right up there with him in high esteem as far as the people go around here. But that doesn't mean squat if you finagle a way to set that Thigpen boy free. I've heard from people right in your office that you don't think he did it."

"Tom, I'm just not convinced…"

The mayor turned to Blake and set upon him with an unwavering stare. "I don't give a good god damn what *you* think, Chief, but losing the coach's daughter like that, all mutilated and such, is the worst thing to ever happen in this town. Now hear me and hear me good, boy. Don't disappoint Coach and Beulah. You nail this son-of-a bitch so the town can get this all behind it and say that justice is done."

Blake's neck began to seethe under his collar, but he maintained his composure, stirring his coffee slowly. "I will thank you, Mayor, to refrain from swearing in the presence of my daughter. I will also thank you to allow me to do my job. I don't know whether the boy is guilty or not, but I will not allow the town to convict Jake before he has his day in court."

The mayor scowled at Blake, then leaned around him to look at Starr. "Forgive me, little lady. But I have few subtle qualities when it comes to my discontentment about things."

"Is that supposed to be an apology, Tom?"

McCown took a sip of his coffee and slammed the mug down hard on the counter top, attracting the attention of everyone else in the diner. "I'm trying to work with you here, Blake. Let me put this all in perspective for you. You work for this town. Hell, you work for *me*. Don't force me to sponsor another candidate to put up before town council next year, boy. But I guaran-damn-tee you that if Thigpen skates, I won't have to. They'll drop you like a hot potato. Now I expect you to lay out everything you come up with to the GBI, your suspicions, your evidence, everything. Then get the hell out of their way. You savvy?"

Blake did not respond.

McCown gave Blake a burning five second stare, then spun around and dismounted his stool, stopping to shake hands with an elderly couple on his way out the door.

"Well," said Katie in a pretend huff. "Looks like our mayor skipped out without paying for his coffee. Guess the Arsh Taters are out as well."

The County Solicitor did charge Jake Thigpen with Marcie's murder and the boy was bound over for a hearing scheduled in mid-July. As hot as this summer was, it was soon fixing to boil over.

Tommy sat mulling over his next move as Starr had just put his king in check.

"Don't sit there all day, Tommy Lee. Do something. You're about two moves from checkmate, anyway."

"Okay, okay. How can I concentrate with you jabberin' all durin' the game? Can we talk about somethin' besides the murders? It gives me the creeps."

"And what else is there to talk about around this town?"

Tommy leaned back in his chair. "I don't know. What about the weirdo? What did your dad do with all the newspaper stuff we copied?"

"Beats me. I haven't seen the articles since he blew up at me over at your house."

"You been watchin' the old guy lately?"

"Everyday. Some days he just stands on the back

deck looking at his yard. Then sometimes he stands at the dining room window for twenty minutes at a time looking straight out with those zombie eyes. But all he can see is the side of our house."

"Maybe he's tryin' to see you walkin' around in your underwear," Tommy giggled, pointing a menacing finger. "I see you, little girl. Hooooo."

"That's not a bit funny, you stupid jerk." With one sweep of her hand she knocked over the remaining pieces.

"Hey! You just forfeited," Tommy said gleefully. "I finally beat you."

Starr flared her nostrils and squinted snidely. "Grow up, Tommy Lee. Just grow up." She jumped up from her chair and moved across the room to her dad's old Army trunk at the foot of her bed. Sitting cross-legged on the floor, she pushed open the lid. Tommy joined her on the floor.

"What are you after?" he asked.

"Nothing really. I just go through this stuff every once in a while."

"What *is* all that?"

Starr took out a manila envelope and dumped the contents on the floor. There were several black and white photos of a teenage girl and a color photo of the same older girl in a wedding dress. Her face was radiant and her red, shoulder length hair, even more brilliant. A younger Blake Ravenel stood beside her in a tuxedo, smiling.

"That's your mom, isn't it? I've never seen a picture of her before. She was real pretty."

Starr nodded and ran her fingers over her mother's face. She knew Tommy could see that her mom was very pregnant on her wedding day and was grateful to Tommy that he did not comment.

"What's that?" He had caught sight of something red and white deeper in the trunk.

"It's Annie." She pulled out a 13 inch Raggedy Ann doll.

"Geez. It's one of those dolls. Where did you get it?"

"My mom got it for me when I was a baby." She pulled it tightly into her chest.

"Kind of freaky to see one of those things, considerin' they've been turn'n up on dead women." He scooted away from the doll as though he didn't want to get close to it.

Starr held it out within a foot of Tommy's face. "She won't bite. See, no teeth." She touched the smiling mouth and giggled.

"Yeah. Very funny. Why do you keep it in that trunk?"

"I don't know. Always have, I guess. It's just where I keep all the things that are important to me. Things that belonged to my mother. Look. These are the pearls that my mom wore at the wedding and this box here has some of her other jewelry in it. Look at these big hoop earrings." She held them against her ear lobes. "Can you imagine anybody wearing something like this? Gaudy, huh? I think maybe my mom was a hippie."

Starr put everything away except the rag doll which

she set on the dresser against the mirror. "There you go, Annie. Now everyone can see your smile."

The Independence Day Parade went on as planned as did the afternoon town barbeque and Liberty Dance at the American Legion Hall later that evening. Besides the Pine River police and county deputies, others were in uniform as well. The Scouts, both boy and girl, marched in the parade behind the Georgia Southern University band and members of the VFW who had donned remnants of their WWII, Korea and Vietnam uniforms walked in route step, waiving at town folk who lined both sides of Main Street.

It was sort of understood that Blake would be Katie's date for the dance, but when he did not pick her up within a half hour of start time, seven-thirty, she went on with Tommy Lee. Around eight-fifteen, however, Blake, in his dress uniform, trim and handsome, did appear at the double doors with Starr. Spying Katie, slow-dancing with her eleven-year old son, Blake moved through the awkward line-dancing bubbas and would be Daisy Dukes and tapped Tommy Lee's shoulder.

"May I cut in, young man?"

Katie gave Blake a chiding look. "Well. I was beginning to wonder if you'd show up tonight."

"Where else would I be? Couldn't miss a chance to dance with the best looking babe in South Georgia. Hope your beau here won't be jealous."

"I guess he won't mind me dumping him. It won't be

the first time I ended up with someone else other than the boy who brought me."

Blake moved in and took her right hand with his left, then placed his right in the small of her back. Her Halston smelled delicious. The blonde hair pulled back in a pony tail made her look eighteen again. Well maybe twenty-five. The shimmering red skirt was tight and her shapely calves made the Tony Lamas look like fashionable western Gucci's. After years of dancing around one another, for the second time in as many weeks, the two former sweethearts now danced together in each others' arms. This left Starr and Tommy Lee standing in the middle of the huge pine floor just looking at one another.

"Well don't just stand there, start dancing," Starr said, hands on hips.

"With you?"

"No. With old Mrs. Worthington over there in the wheelchair. Of course me, Simpleton."

"I...I never learned to dance. Anyway, it'd be like dancin' with my sister."

"You were dancing with your mother, weren't you? Come on, limber up," she said, grabbing both hands. "You're as stiff as a two by four."

The Dixie Johns were playing the event. They were just two local singers named John who scraped together two other guys to back them up and their repertoire of George Jones, Charlie Rich and Johnny Cash songs. They weren't bad, either, most people thought. Over the steel guitar, bass and drums a half dozen loud and animated voices could be heard near the bar. Two of Blake's and two of Bobby's teammates were arguing over which state championship team, 1968 or 1970, was the better.

"Five turnovers all season and only one lead to a score. Your 1970 team had three times the turnovers and over half ended up in the other team scoring. And then the '70 team was scored on more times and lost two regular season games. We went undefeated." Scoop Cunningham knew his stats.

"Now ah moan tell ya'll the real differnce. We outscored your '68 team two hunnert and ninety points to your two-ten," replied Ray Boy Skaggs.

"Only because most of your competition had no defense. Not one of the other teams placed a defensive player on the All-State squad. Not even honorable mention," Scoop shot back.

Blake came up behind the bragging beer swillers and placed one each hand on the shoulders of his teammates. "Too bad Coach is not here tonight, boys. He'd tell you girls on the '70 team there never was nor will ever be as great a team as what we put on the field."

Bobby stepped in, playfully squaring off to Blake. "But you gotta admit, Blake old man, our cheerleaders were better looking."

"Now wait a minute, Bobby Zale," piped in a less than sober Carter Culbreath. "I married one of them '68 cheerleaders."

Bobby winked at Blake. "I rest my case."

Within a few moments, the men became silent and

stoic, staring into their plastic beer cups. The one face, a face that had not missed a Fourth of July dance in over twenty years, was Coach St. Clair's. They missed him and hurt deeply for him.

Blake spoke up after a while. "I'm going over to check on Coach in a few minutes. Anybody want to ride over with me? I'd like to think he'd enjoy our company tonight. Maybe just for a few minutes?"

As the word had spread rapidly though the hall, everyone there who had ever played for The Saint agreed to go. The married ex-jocks told their wives they would be back before the end of the dance and not one of the women objected under the circumstances. Coach St. Clair was as much an icon to them as to their men. Blake asked Katie to take Starr home with her and when he returned, they would all watch the fireworks from her front porch at ten.

Charlie St. Clair was visibly moved when his front yard floodlight illuminated the faces of no less than twenty-five of his former players from 1962 on. "For you boys to come out here as a group like this, it….it just stirs my heart. I know we saw one another at Marcie's wake…" He stopped to swallow hard and wipe his eyes. "…but you breakin' from your families and sharin' with me the day that we all hold special, it makes me proud to have been your coach."

The visit did much to lift everyone's spirit, including the St. Clairs. As the line of taillights finally streamed away from the house and down Sydenstricker toward the highway, Charlie drew Beulah in close with his huge bear-like arm. Though their hearts still hemorrhaged, they managed their first smiles since the evening before Marcie Rose disappeared from their world forever.

On the morning of the fifth, Blake sat slumped in his leather desk chair with his eyes closed and fingertips against the bridge of his nose. Mental pictures of Marcie's face, sweet smile and laughing eyes, intermingled with images of Starr and Katie, the two most precious people in his life. He shuddered just to think any harm would ever come to either of them. Opening his eyes to reach out for the telephone to call Starr, he was startled to see the haggard face of Bessie Cotter in the doorway. She stood for a moment without speaking, her haunting stare almost piercing his soul. Then stepped further into his office.

"Weren't no one out front. Sorry if I skeered you."

"No. No. Come on in Mrs. Cotter." Blake replied, rising to his feet. "Please have a seat."

She shook her head and looked around the room, anxiously.

"Can I help you?"

"Got some place to spit?" She pointed to her lower lip.

Bessie's need to dump her Skoal didn't immediately register with Blake, but then the alarm went off in his eyes and he moved quickly to place his trash can in her hands. With one finger she dug out the patch of snuff and spit twice in the can. "Wanted to tell you somethin.' That depitty of yours, the young one who came out the other day to ask me about the St. Clair girl....if I saw her the night when…you know."

"Yes."

"Well I didn't, mind you. Told him as much. But what I forgot to tell him was that I heered a car and when I looked out my winder, saw a big black vee-hicle under the streetlight with no lights on it, movin' slow."

"What kind of vehicle, Mrs. Cotter?"

"A Chevy. That's what it was. One of them SUV types."

"You're sure about the make?"

"I may be a loony old hag like everyone says, but I know my makes, Chief. My boy Russell was in used cars and I learned them all. Ain't no other woman in this town knows more about makes."

"Where did it go?"

"It just went down toward the coach's house and I didn't see it no more after that."

"If that seemed suspicious to you, why didn't you call us?"

"Pretty hard to do when you ain't got no phone."

"Could you make out the driver?"

"Nope. Too dark. Anyways, I could see that the truck had blacked out winders."

Blake stroked his chin and reflected on the woman. The first real clue and it had to come from a woman some referred to as crazy, senile and even possessed. But he believed she saw what she saw.

"Mrs. Cotter, do you know the boy, Jake Thigpen?"

"Yeah, I know who he is. Know his mom, too."

"Did you see him or his car the night Marcie St. Clair was….was killed?"

"No. But I heered that old Camaro of his'n down by the hard road. It never came by my place."

"You're sure."

"I said it, didn't I?" She appeared agitated and Blake sensed it.

"Okay, Mrs. Cotter. I do appreciate what you're telling me. Is there anything else you can remember?"

She shook her head. "Gotta go. Russell's waitin' on me out in the truck."

"Thank you, ma'am, for coming in. Your information will be a big help." He walked her to the door. "If you can think of anything else…"

"I told you all I know and that's the end of it," she said, gruffly.

"Yes, ma'am."

Blake returned to his office and scribbled down '*black Chevy SUV. Suburban? Possibly blacked out windows. Did anyone else see it? Check out.*' How many black Suburbans were there in the Pine River area or Savannah for that matter, Blake thought. He did know one thing: there was a strange bird living next door to him who also had a black Suburban. And Blake had seen the man come home from somewhere not too long after ten o'clock on the Saturday night Marcie St. Clair was murdered.

"Did you not hear the phone, Chief?" Anna Mae stood in Blake's doorway with her thumb and pinky extended in opposite directions by her ear.

Blake wheeled his chair around. "What? Sorry. Guess I was a million miles away. I didn't realize you had come in. Who is it?"

"A Captain Bannister."

Blake leaned over, tapped the lighted button on the phone with his finger and picked up the receiver. "Blake Ravenel."

"Hello, Chief. This is Bill Bannister at the Trenton, NJ Police Department. How are you doing today?"

"Fine, Captain. Yes, I was told about you."

"Yeah, I wanted to let you know I looked over the sketch your daughter drew of the man she thinks is my murder suspect. I think it's a good composite of what Morris could look like now. Good aging job. When she grows up and ever wants to work as a police artist, we could sure use her. We're impressed up here."

"I'm very proud of Starr, Captain. So you think this is a possible match."

"I think there is a strong resemblance. I got to tell you, pal; I had only been a detective a couple of years when Morris killed his wife and children. The most horrific thing I ever saw. It's haunted the hell out of me these years. Every once in a while someone sends me a lead, but it never proves out."

"I assume you have Morris' fingerprints on file and some physical evidence samples?" posed Blake.

"Yeah, except forensic science was not then what it is now. We do have some bloody finger and shoe prints which checked out to be his. Can we bring your man in for fingerprints?"

"I don't know if all this is enough to establish probable cause. He doesn't *have* to submit to fingerprinting, but maybe there's another way. If we can get them, we'll send them up."

"Appreciate what you can do. If this case would ever resolve, I believe I'd go ahead and retire. I'd be a happy man, Chief."

"Will do what we can, sir. Thanks."

Bobby came on shift at ten and as soon as Blake heard his voice, he asked him to step in.

"Yeah, Blake?"

"Go pick up the man that lives on my right, Rupert Kolb."

"What's the deal? Has he done something?"

"He may be a suspect in a murder investigation up in New Jersey. And Bessie Cotter saw a black Suburban like Kolb has going down Sydenstricker sometime after Jake Thigpen said he left Marcie rose."

"Damn, Blake. Thigpen's as guilty as sin. Do we need another suspect to muddy the waters?"

"I'm just keeping an open mind on our investigation and exploring all possibilities."

"Okay, "Bobby sighed. "I'll get him."

"And Bobby. Be gentle. Don't tell him anything or read him his rights. Just say I'd like to talk to him."

Bobby donned his cap. "Be back in a few minutes."

In less than twenty minutes a very angry Rupert Kolb entered the station house door. Bobby's fingertips were edging him forward and into Blake's office.

"Good morning, Mr. Kolb. Please come in and sit down. Thank you for agreeing to be here." He extended his hand to greet the man, but Kolb ignored it and sat down in the chair opposite the chief's desk. He said nothing as well and instead fixed his cold eyes onto Blake's.

Blake began. "Mr. Kolb, you've lived next door to me for more than three years now and I know we haven't had much dialogue. And I'm sorry about that."

"You place me under arrest because we didn't make friends?'

"No, no. You're not under arrest, sir. I just needed to ask you a few questions."

Kolb's penetrating stare was unwavering. "And you couldn't just come next door to talk to me. You had to send your man here to get me and treat me like a common criminal."

"Mr. Kolb, how about a cup of coffee. Bobby, would you get him one?"

Before Kolb could say 'yes' or 'no', Bobby poured out a

cup and shoved it in the man's hand. Kolb appeared rather annoyed at this and did not immediately take a sip.

"I did have some questions for you, Mr. Kolb, that served better being asked here."

"Then get on with it." Kolb finally put the cup to his lips, took a drink and frowned. "I suppose you call this coffee."

Blake cleared his throat and glanced at the pot of black nastiness. He turned his eyes back to Kolb. "You know what has happened right here in our community over the past few weeks. The two murders, that is."

Kolb shifted in his chair. "And naturally you think I would be a perfect suspect."

"You're not a suspect, Mr. Kolb, but we have a witness who saw a black Chevy Suburban like yours near the scene of the last murder…and on the same night."

Kolb's eyes softened a little, but remained on Blake's. "I'm sure there are scores of black Suburbans within fifty miles of here. How many of those owners have you brought in here?

"You're the first."

"I thought as much," Kolb shot back, sarcastically. "Guess I was a *convenient* suspect."

"I didn't say you were a suspect. Do you consider yourself one?"

Kolb's expression reflected that he did not want to dignify the question with a response. "And where exactly was this vehicle supposed to be?"

"Near the murder scene, as I said. You don't know

where that was? If you don't, then you're the only person in this town that doesn't."

"Mr. Ravenel, as you know, I'm a very private person. I don't make it my business to gossip and I don't listen to it. All I know is a young girl was murdered. The high school coach's daughter I hear. And I don't know any more about the thing than what I read in the paper."

"You remember the Saturday night it happened? The second one in June?"

"I remember."

"I saw you pulling into your driveway about eleven-thirty that night. Do you mind telling me where you had been?"

"Don't you think that's my business?" The ire in Kolb's voice intensified.

"It will be *official* business if you don't tell me, sir." Blake tried to read the man to determine if he was intentionally equivocating or just plain arbitrary.

"If you must know, I was in Savannah visiting someone."

"Will that *someone* verify you were there?"

"He will."

Blake took from his pocket a small notepad. "His name, if you don't mind."

As much as Kolb showed he hated being grilled, he answered in resignation. "A priest. Father Mario at St. John the Baptist. You can check it out. I was there till about nine."

"Perhaps I will, Mr. Kolb. Were you anywhere near Sydenstricker Road and 41 that night?"

"That's three or four miles south of here. I just told you I was in Savannah. That's north, if I remember my Geography."

Blake's face broadcast his annoyance with Kolb's tart responses, but then again, he realized this was in keeping with the man's personality. He paused without word for a few moments to give Kolb some of his own 'stare-down' medicine. Finally, he broke the ice. "Okay, Mr. Kolb, that's all for now. You can go."

As Kolb set the coffee cup on the carpet and stood to leave, Blake stopped him. "Wait. There is one more question. Who is Bonnie Wagner?"

Kolb who still stood with his back to Blake preparing to exit the room, turned slowly. "I see that you actually *are* investigating me, Chief. So, what do you think you know about me?"

"I don't know. *You* tell *me*."

Kolb placed his hands in his pockets and scowled, menacingly. "I lived with the woman for over ten years in her apartment. Then she died. She willed me her car and some money and I moved out of state. Simple as that."

"But, Mr. Kolb, there's no record of you as a resident anywhere in New Jersey. That *is* where you came from?"

"You know very well it is. I never owned any property or a car there. Lived in New York before that. Are we done here, Chief?"

"What do you do, Mr. Kolb?"

"Nothing. Done nothing for more than twenty years. I've been disabled all that time."

"I see." Blake was out of buttons to push. "Okay. That's it, sir. Bobby, would you take Mr. Kolb home?"

Kolb pulled his hands from his pockets and gave Blake a parting shot. And an even deeper stare. "I'll walk. And Chief, the next time you want to chit-chat, be a neighbor. Come to my house and treat me like somebody who lives in this town. Say hello once in a while, if you can manage it."

Blake wasn't sure if he was feeling guilty or gullible. He had never reached out to be friendly to the man, but Kolb just always seemed to be someone he wouldn't necessarily want to befriend. Blake watched him limp and drag the game foot down Main Street until he disappeared from sight.

Questions still loomed in Blake's mind. If Kolb lived in New Jersey for ten years or more, whether or not he owned a car, he drew disability and the feds would have a record of that. How did he become disabled? Why did he decide on living in podunk Pine River?

Blake sat on the edge of his desk eyeing the coffee cup on the floor by the chair. If Kolb had been sitting in a confessional as late as nine that Saturday night, he would still have been back in Pine River in ample time to drive to the opposite side of town, commit the murder and be in his driveway at the time Blake saw him pull in. But how would Kolb know where Marcie was at the very time she was abandoned by Thigpen and just happen to catch her walking down Sydenstricker? Jake had said that Marcie thought she had heard something or someone in the bushes just after they made love. The lake was just off 17 and on Kolb's way back from Savannah. Kolb could have seen the parked Camaro, trailed off into the woods to watch the lovers devour each other and then follow them.

But for some intuitive reason, Blake couldn't see Kolb as the killer. Odd? Eccentric? Mysterious? All of the above for sure. Blake always considered himself a good judge of men. He just couldn't put Rupert Kolb at the scene of Marcie's murder. Jake was a 'slam dunk' for everyone in town except Blake and the boy's mother. But if Kolb was to be a suspect, was there any circumstantial evidence against him besides the Suburban? And then there was the credibility of Bessie Cotter about the Suburban in the first place. So Kolb was with a priest at a late hour on a Saturday night. Why? Most probably to ask forgiveness of the sins he had committed. Or could it be to ask forgiveness for a sin he was about to commit?

Blake lifted the coffee cup from the floor by spreading out his fingers on the inside of the mug. After pouring out the remaining contents, he dropped it into a plastic evidence bag. Tomorrow the GBI would have the mysterious Rupert Kolb's fingerprints. Would he be Bannister's long-sought killer, Stanley Morris, or would he have any record at all?

CHAPTER EIGHT

Starr and her dad sat in lawn chairs on their backyard brick patio taking in the sweet aroma of gardenias that lined the fence between the Ravenel and Kolb houses. With heads laid back and faces cranked high toward a blackboard sky filled with diamond-like stars, they listened to the music of the night. The tree frogs and crickets were in full voice. The humidity of the day was gone and the unusual radiational cooling in the dead of summer made it a perfect evening for star gazing. A fingernail moon that lay off the eastern horizon added no illumination, allowing the night sky appear all the more brilliant.

"There's Cassiopeia," Blake said, pointing. He could not help but become interested in the heavens over the years. Although he had learned to navigate at night by the stars in Ranger School, he actually learned more about them in Vietnam from his platoon leader, Lieutenant Anderson. Anderson was an Astronomy major at the

University of Colorado and had talked with Blake many times about his job offer from the Palomar Conservatory where he was anxious to go to work the day after his separation from the Army. On many vivid starlit nights when the NVA was not on the move, the lieutenant educated his sergeant on all the constellations, singling out specific stars, their locations and distances. It all may have later meant less to him had the young officer not been found by a sniper's bullet, ending his life only a week before he was to rotate back to 'the World.' Blake vowed on that traumatic day that he would not only take home the knowledge that had been passed on to him, but to teach the night sky to his daughter as well.

"Daddy, did Mom study the stars like you?"

"Actually, she got into star gazing long before I ever did. After you were born, she would bring you out on this very spot and tell you about the stars. You would lie in your bassinette, watch them twinkle, and listen to her like you knew exactly what she was talking about. Your eyes would dart all over the sky in wonderment and your mom would smile that pretty smile of hers. She loved you so much. She even picked out a star and told you that it was yours."

A wide grin broke out on Starr's face. "Which one was that?"

"I'm not sure. You know, I'm ashamed to say I didn't pay much attention back then. But why don't you go ahead now and choose one?"

"Okay, I think I'll choose *that* one." She pointed

to a particularly glistening star. "That's Betelgeuse, you know."

Blake smiled and nodded. "So that settles it. From this day forth it will have a new name: *Betelgeuse Starr.* Starr with two r's."

It had been another special evening for Starr. Of course, *any* night was a good night when she and her father sat around talking and he actually opened up to tell her something about her mother she didn't know.

Suddenly, the phone rang and Starr jumped up to go inside to answer it. "That's probably Tommy Lee. I think he's mad because I didn't go over there to play that stupid Atari game."

But it wasn't Tommy. "Hey, Starbright, is your dad around?"

"Hi, Bobby," she answered in her twelve-year old sexy voice. "Are you sure it's not me you want to talk to?"

Bobby laughed. "Some other time, kiddo. Put your dad on."

Blake picked up on the kitchen phone. "What's up?"

"The Thigpen boy tried to hang himself tonight at County lockup."

"What? Is he all right?"

"Yeah. They took him to St. Theresa's for observation. One of the deputies found him. He had taken a bed sheet and knotted it, tied one end around his neck and the other up high on the window bars, then jumped. They say he's critical, but should make it."

"Damn," sighed Blake.

"That ought to tell you something, Chief. He doesn't want to live with all that guilt. Guess he knows he'll fry and probably wanted to take the easy way out."

"Yeah, maybe. All right. Thanks, man. Linc will be on in a few minutes to relieve you. Go get some sleep."

When Blake hung up, Starr came into the kitchen. "That's awful, Dad."

"You were listening? You know better than that, Starr. What conversations I have with my officers, you're not to hear. Police business is not for your ears, understand?"

"Yes, Daddy."

"Time for bed, Starbright. Get on up to your room."

It was nearly four and sticky hot the next Thursday afternoon. It was yet another one of those heavy, breath-sapping summer days in South Georgia when the atmosphere is still and the temperature is well above 95 degrees. Blake's shirt was actually soaked from sweat to a point where his military creases had long since wilted. Off to the southwest the sky had darkened and flashes of distant lightning reflected off the aluminum roof of the Kincaid Building. Rumbles of thunder followed each radiant flash within increasingly shorter intervals. Thunderstorms always took Blake back a dozen years before when the sky lit up some nights from artillery barrages or Arc Light strikes. He would count the seconds between flash and bang to determine how close they were to his position.

Blake threw open the door to the station house and

stepped into what felt like a meat locker. A blast of cold air almost immediately chilled him to the bone. "Is it cold enough in here for everybody!" he yelled.

Anna Mae smiled and retorted, "Well, *I'm* comfortable."

"Is any body not watching the weather? We're fixing to get a good one." Blake reached up to turn on the office TV and rotated the dial to Channel Seven. It always gave the best storm coverage.

Immediately, four piercing signals preceded a special weather statement that ran across the bottom of the screen. An advancing cold front had rocketed through Alabama and the Atlanta area earlier, spawning a series of super cells, now making Savannah and surrounding burgs its next target. A tornado warning had been issued for Liberty and McIntosh Counties as an F3 twister had already touched down between the towns of Midway and Crossroads. Pine River was in its path.

At ten after four, Chief Whitaker at the fire station called Anna Mae to alert the department that he would be sounding the Tornado Warning siren imminently.

Blake then called his house to warn Starr. "You know what to do. Watch the sky and trees and if the wind suddenly picks up, head for the basement."

Within mere minutes the lightning was fierce and the thundering booms began rattling the windows. The people that remained in the streets were now scurrying into buildings and cars. Skirts were being blown up and brand new hairdos from Mabel's were ruined by the wind now gusting over thirty-five mph. Suddenly the red and white awning from the State Farm office across from the station tore loose and disappeared over the building's rooftop.

Blake positioned Linc at the fire station and told Anna Mae to call the off-duty Bobby to begin patrolling the streets in his squad car. On the TV, the EBS again sounded its four obnoxious blares. The message followed:

This is a special weather bulletin from the Emergency Broadcast System. A tornado warning has been issued for the following locations: McIntosh, Crossroads, Pine River, Richmond Hill and the City of Savannah. At four-thirty two pm a tornado was confirmed on the ground in Long County moving to the east northeast at thirty miles per hour....

Blake grabbed his yellow rain slicker and bull horn, told Anna Mae to crouch down under the desk should the storm hit the station, and went outside onto Main Street to assure all town folk were off the street. Keying his shoulder mike, he yelled into it above the intense wind, "This is Ravenel! Radio check! Come in!"

Both Bobby and Linc responded "Loud and clear!"

"Stay vigilant out there, fellows! The storm is upon us and we'll be getting a lot of calls."

As suddenly as the wind had come up, it died to a dead calm. Blake had experienced several such storms in the past and he knew this was a super cell's trick to fool everyone into believing the worst had passed them by. But the western sky had a green cast to it. The color of trouble. The atmospheric turbulence and drop in barometric pressure actually made it difficult for Blake to breathe. Then he saw it. A huge thunderhead. And from out of that cell a V-shaped funnel cloud with a black edge appeared over the New Life Church on Stewart Street, suddenly dipping down toward the roof. The small, white church with its ornate bell tower and skyline spire then exploded in thousands of pieces, some of which were caught up in the spinning cloud like matchsticks.

Blake raised the bullhorn to his mouth and shouted, "Everybody off the street! Get inside away from the windows and into an inner room!"

It was obvious to Blake that the funnel cloud would catch at least a portion of the downtown area. To his horror, directly in the tornado's path, was the frail, eighty-two year old Virginia Riley, his third grade schoolteacher, moving ever too slowly toward her Valiant. "Mrs. Riley!" Blake called. "Stay there! Don't get into your car! I'll come and get you!" Apparently she did not hear him and continued taking her baby steps with the aid of her cane.

Like a sprinter out of starting blocks, Blake ran to her. Sweeping her up under his right arm as though she were a football, he dashed back toward the block station house and deposited her inside. When she had regained her faculties, Mrs. Riley then began giving him the devil for man-handling her like he did. "And to think I supported you getting this job. Shame on you, Blake Ravenel."

Within a matter of seconds the twister ripped through Noble's Antique Shop and picked up Mrs. Riley's Valiant, slamming it into the drive-through window at the C&S Bank. *Thank God*, he thought, that most of town's patrons had heeded the warnings and vacated the streets. Even as the tornado was still working over the northeast end of town near the water tower, Blake was back on the street, running from building to building. At the same time he was barking into his radio for Linc and Bobby to check for any casualties where they were situated. All the while he prayed that Starr, Katie and Tommy Lee were okay.

The twister, which had decimated five businesses in town, wreaked moderate damage to dozens of others. Oaks and pines lay across streets and onto houses. Power lines were down all over town and the water tower was no longer visible over the middle school. Linc, who had escorted the rescue squad to the trailer park where the Thigpens lived, or now *used* to live, radioed Blake. "A lot of cuts and bruises, but miraculously, nobody killed. Hell, man, God must hate mobile home parks. Every time a tornado touches down, that's the first thing it hits. Looks like a war zone out here."

"Not much better here in town," echoed Blake. "There may be a lot of damage, but appears we dodged the bullet on injuries and deaths."

By five-thirty the sky had lightened and the rain stopped. Blake knew it would be a long night, not only for him, but the folks from GEMA, the power crews and the cable guys. He then asked Anna Mae to take Mrs. Riley home. When she went out and saw her demolished Valiant sticking out of the teller window, she turned sheepishly to her Chief and said, "Thank you, Blake. You're a good boy. I won't be forgetting you saving my life today." She then stood up on her toes and kissed him on the forehead.

Blake locked up the station and drove by his house to check on Starr. Upon hearing his vehicle, she came running down the sidewalk. "I'm okay. I'm okay! I went to the basement like you said. But look. There's a tree on our house." Blake saw that that the huge sixty foot oak in their back yard had uprooted and laid itself into the roof over Starr's bedroom.

"I'm taking you over to Katie's, Starr. You can stay there tonight if it's okay with her. I have to get back up town, now."

As business owners began showing up to assess the damage to their buildings, Blake called Scooter's Wrecker Service to pull the Valiant out of the bank. He would have to stay close until emergency repairs were made to the building. Any unapproved withdrawals were the last thing the citizens of Pine River wanted. Enough money would be leaving their hands as it was, especially from those who were underinsured. As the wrecker was working the car loose, a teenage looter apparently thought Blake was too occupied to notice him stepping out of Burt's TV and Appliance broken storefront window, cradling a 19 inch Magnavox. Unfortunately for him, Blake was standing within ten feet of the store with his arms folded, sporting a piercing stare.

"Put down the TV and place your hands behind your head."

But the boy panicked, dropped the set, splattering pieces on the sidewalk like shrapnel, and hot-footed away.

"Stop right there!" Blake called, pulling out his nightstick. But the boy continued on down Main. As though it were 1968 again and the Rebels' All-State quarterback was throwing down-field to a receiver, Blake side-armed his billy club twenty yards in the air, allowing it to skip along the sidewalk another ten, and tripping up the thief, bringing him hard to the pavement. Wrecker man Scooter Claiborne, himself a former Rebel nose guard in the Fifties, whooped, "Damn! Still got that golden arm, Chief!"

Blake then detected a noise inside the appliance store. Spotting an obvious second looter through the open pane, he pulled his Glock and called out. "Come on out here now!" The kid, no more than sixteen and scared to death that Blake was going to fire, gave up without incident. And the break-away robber that Blake tagged on the street only suffered a lacerated chin and skinned elbows where he banged the sidewalk. Otherwise, he was in good enough shape to join his partner-in- crime in the station jail.

Starr had to move downstairs temporarily to the previously unused bedroom until the contractors repaired the roof and ceiling. One of the trusses had to be replaced as did some of the naughty pine in her room. On the second day of repairs, the foreman, Julio Garcia, called from the top of the stairs to Starr, telling her that he had found something. Wedged in an angle of the storm-damaged truss was a small black book that appeared to be some type of diary covered in cobwebs. "Miss Starr, it looks like someone went though the access door to your storage area and hid it up there. Probably wanted to be sure no one would find it. I don't think it would be yours because the pages are all yellow. Must have been there for years."

She thanked Julio and took the book into the parlor to examine it. It had writing inside. Pages of it. She knew her grandmother had bought the house some time in the mid 1960s. Maybe it was hers. Maybe she had kept it since she was a young girl and finally decided to bury it in the attic when she knew she was dying. Then again, perhaps it belonged to some tormented little girl like Anne Frank who poured out her very soul about some horrific experience. The adrenaline raced in Starr's veins in anticipation about what she would find. A piece of history uncovered. She kicked her shoes off and tucked her legs up under her on the sofa. The diary smelled musty and its faded cover appeared to have been baked by years of 120 degree heat below the roof. Tenderly, she opened the cover to read the first page:

I think the last time I had a diary was when I was eight. I was in love with Jimmy Cominsky in the third grade. After school I couldn't wait to get home and write down everything he said and did that day. He had given me a Valentine that year which had the word 'love' in it and then he told me he wanted to be my boyfriend. It was the Valentine's Day I will remember the rest of my life. He was the first boy I ever loved. But that was 1958 and the romance was over in May when school was out and I fell in love with Billy Cobb....

Starr was now intrigued. So it was 1958, she thought. It was definitely someone who lived in the house before her dad and grandma moved in.

...I had a few boyfriends over the years. It was all very innocent. When I was fifteen I remember it was the first real time I thought about having sex with a boy. It was Kenny Damron. He swept me off my feet and made me feel real special. He even told me he loved me one night when we were skating over at Dreamland. I filled up a dozen pages in my diary after I got home. The very next day I overheard him tell another boy outside the gym that he told me that because he wanted to get into my pants. He was actually interested in Janie Moore. I was crushed. I guess it was payback for me dumping Jimmy Cominsky. That was the last entry in that diary. I had it for over seven years. It just seemed fitting to splash lighter fluid on it and set fire to it in my back yard.

But I guess I was still a child then and really didn't experience love (at least that's what I thought it was) until I met Blake.

Starr's heart skipped a beat and she suddenly felt she could not get her breath. She fanned her flushed face with the First Baptist Church fan-on-a-stick and whispered through her swelling throat, "My mother's diary."

She read on:

I had just moved to town and saw Blake for the first time at a dance. He was strong and handsome, maybe the best looking boy in Pine River with his dark, healthy head of hair and deep blue eyes. All the girls went for him and why not? He was the star quarterback, scouted by all the colleges, and was going places. But he had dated Katie, the school darling, and nobody had a chance with him. But then they broke up when she went away to college. He may not have realized it, but I actually arranged for us to be at Lonesome Bill's at the same time. That's when I decided to get my hooks in him. Latching onto Blake also got me away from someone who at the time I thought was a creep and who was obsessed with me, but who later I found so different.

But I always thought I was Blake's rebound girl and he never really loved me like he loved Katie Hill. I resented that and after feeling it day in and day out, I suppose it pretty much killed my feelings for him. But then, wouldn't you know it; I found out I was pregnant…

When Starr read the next few lines, huge teardrops rolled down her cheeks and splashed onto the pages, smudging the ink.

…I wanted to have an abortion right away, but Blake got really pissed. He got in my face and said 'you will not kill our baby.' I hated him for saying it like that. I hated him for us being in that predicament.

Six months later we got married. It was a cold marriage right from the beginning. I thought of it as more of an arrangement or a 'have-to' marriage.

Then Starr was born. She is a precious little thing. She

has changed my whole attitude about being a mother and I had regretted ever having thoughts about disposing of her. If it hadn't been for her, I would've walked. Of course I wouldn't have gotten married in the first place..."

Tears continued forming in Starr's eyes. She slammed the diary to the floor and walked to the tall parlor window. For a moment she closed her eyes and took in a deep breath. Tilting back her head, she opened them to look in the direction of the white humid sky. Was her mother up there somewhere looking down on her? Somehow, in reading the diary of her very own mother, for the first time in her life she actually felt close to her. It was as though Luann Ravenel was somehow communicating with her through a stroke of fate, uncovered by a tornado. But whatever she was feeling about her mother, it was mixed with anger and confusion. This was not the woman's face in the wedding photo. That face was happy and it had painted an image in Starr's mind of a mother who loved her father. And had she not died, they would have been a storybook family. Starr may have been feeling her mother's presence through the diary, but at that moment she never felt so alone.

Her eyes dropped from above the trees and into the dining room window next door. There, staring a hole right though her, were the icy cold eyes of the ogre, Rupert Kolb. Starr jumped back and let out a slight cry, much like a small bird. From the shadows of the parlor she could still see the man standing still, stoic, almost trance-like, hands in pockets. A chill ran through the back of Starr's neck, causing her to shiver. This could be the man who killed his family, two of which were young girls just like her. If he could do that to his wife and children, he could so easily snuff out her life for being a snoop and a meddler.

Rupert Kolb's face and Luann Ravenel's diary were entirely too much for her that afternoon. Although still confined to the house for her own safety, she had to flee. Gathering up her bike from the front porch, she bounced it down the steps and into the street. The hot sun on her face and beautiful auburn hair flowing behind her, Starr tried to pound the written words of her mother out of her head through the pedals of her bike. Although the Ravenel and Bledsoe houses were scarcely three blocks apart, she errantly covered more than a dozen streets, finally wheeling into Tommy Lee's front yard. The diary would remain her secret for now, but today she needed the ear of her best friend.

The intercom buzzed on Blake's phone. "Chief, it's Captain Bannister from Trenton," said Anna Mae. "Can you take the call?"

"Yeah. I'll pick up." He and Link exchanged looks of anticipation.

"Yes, sir. Good to hear from you. Did you get the prints?"

"We did, Blake. Unfortunately, the prints do not match those of Stanley Morris. Looks like your Mr. Kolb is not the man we're looking for. Yet another disappointment for us. I guess our case gets shelved again until the next time. I really thought we had something here."

"Sorry, Captain. Not to bring any ill will to my neighbor, but I was hoping he was your man. And if he was, he'd be moving up the food chain on our short list of suspects in our case as well."

When the conversation ended, Linc added, "On the other hand, that don't mean Kolb *ain't* our man."

"For some reason, Linc, I don't think Kolb *or* Thigpen killed Marcie. And I'm thoroughly convinced Jake didn't kill the other three women." Blake shook his head. "Baffling, all right." He then picked up the receiver again and touched one of the outside line buttons. "While I'm thinking about it, I need to call County to see how Jake is."

Starr thought she would be back home before her dad got off duty, but there he was, waiting for her on the front porch when she slid her rear tire into the grass. His eyes said it all, so Starr put on her defense. "I know. I know. You said I couldn't go out biking until further notice, but I just went over to Tommy Lee's. I rode fast and didn't stop to talk to anyone. And I've had a very bad day if you must know. If you must jump on my case, then please get it over with."

Although Blake's face was stern and emotionless, he had to smile inside at Starr's unsolicited soliloquy.

"Supper's on the table," he replied, turning his back. After a moment, the smile was fully evident on his face. He had been more concerned than angry with her. Now, he was just relieved that she was home.

CHAPTER NINE

The next morning Starr made it a point to tell her dad that she would indeed stay home all day and if there were some kind of emergency, she would call him. Not to worry. He nodded and winked. And she *would* stay home all day, too. There was a diary to read and today she was in a more positive and renewed state of mind to get into it.

Blake either seemed to be lollygagging around the kitchen too long or Starr's anticipation to again begin reading her mother's words prompted her to push him out the door. "Daddy, aren't you going to be late for the town council meeting? It's a quarter till nine," she said, glancing at the kitchen clock.

"They won't start without me. By the way, what do you have planned today?"

"Well, they're supposed to finish up my room today, so I guess I'll move some of my things back up. Also, I want to do a little reading."

"I thought you took the summer off from reading. You missing school or something?"

"Just catching up on a little history, that's all?"

"You're not still reading about that murdered New Jersey family, are you? If so, you can take your suspect Mr. Kolb off the list."

"No, I wasn't going to read any more about that, but why do you say he's out as a suspect?" Starr *was* still intrigued about him, but the tornado, her displacement and her mom's diary had more recently occupied her mind.

"We questioned Mr. Kolb, lifted his prints and sent them to the Trenton police. They didn't match the alleged murderer's. But….there's been enough 'murder' talk these last few weeks. Let's not dwell any further on it."

She didn't respond, but her eyes darted in a dozen directions, making it apparent she was digesting the new information.

"Okay, now I *am* late," Blake said, kissing his hand and planting it on Starr's forehead. "See you at supper."

The next several pages of Luann's diary went on about Starr's first year of life, her bright, glimmering eyes, bright as the star she was, and her cute expressions.

She can charm the pants off anyone and I am just bowled over how everyone makes over her…"

About ten pages through, the diary took a dark turn:

…I am as angry with Blake as I have ever been. Maybe

the angriest. He had come to me a few weeks ago, saying he wanted to do something for his country with the war and all, and wanted to enlist in the Army. I thought I had shut that notion down months ago, telling him that Vietnam had enough men fighting its war, and he had a child to be father to. We had the biggest fight about that and he went and joined up anyway. He leaves next Thursday. I told him that Starr and I may not be here when he got back. That is if he makes it back. He got really pissed when I said that and told me maybe he just wouldn't come back.

Much as the day before, the adrenaline rushed and the pounding in Starr's heart was summoned again by her mother's words:

Starr and I went with him to the bus station today. Hardly a word was spoken. I guess we were still mad at one another; I more than him. I stood with Starr in my arms, looking like some forlorn wife in a 1940s World War II movie, watching her husband wave from the back of the bus as he went bravely off to fight the Nazis. Blake is supposed to go to some place in New Jersey, Ft. Dix I think, then on to some Infantry training back here in Georgia and then to paratrooper school. Why in the world he thinks he needs to jump out of airplanes is beyond me. Tonight I am lonelier than I've ever been in my life. If I didn't have Starr, I'd probably jump, myself. Off the Nine Mile Bridge.

Starr laid the diary down and placed her face in her hands. She knew that only a year and a half later, a month or two after her dad came home from Vietnam, her mother's car *did* go off that bridge. Her chest swelled and ached at the horrifying thought. Did her mom take her life or was her death an accident like everybody said?

Luann continued on for several pages, lamenting how alone and sad she was the thirty or so weeks of Blake's training. She saw her father every weekend and spent a few nights up at Lonesome Bill's nursing a few beers. A lot of guys hit on her, but she staved them off. Most of them were creeps anyway.

Blake came home after his Airborne and Ranger courses. Home to hot meals, but unfortunately, a cold wife. In four days he was gone again, this time for at least a year. And this time Luann did not see him off. While Blake was boarding a Flying Tiger at Charleston Air Force Base, bound ultimately for Vietnam, she was helping her dad celebrate his 50th birthday in Savannah.

…I do feel guilty tonight. He really did deserve to be sent off with a fiery night of passion. I probably could have mustered, but unsure if he even wanted to. My body was ready and even willing for his. Guess we both would have felt like hypocrites. Okay, so this was his own choosing to go off from us like this, but I do admire him for his courage and patriotism. I have no f…ing idea why we're even in this war, but since I'm a political illiterate anyway, maybe somebody in Washington knows better than me.

Starr took a moment to digest the words. She knew nothing about the war, except she thought she remembered her dad's ranting back a few years ago when "this country betrayed 58,000 of its dead heroes and guys like me who were fortunate to make it back in one piece." To her

the words in the diary may as well have been written a
hundred years before.

*I saw R again today. (I have to refer to him as R in case
somehow my diary gets away from me). I have a much better
liking for him, now that I've gotten to know him better. He's
sweet, not to mention a great looking guy, and he wants to
take me to dinner. He says he understands that the tongues in
Pine River will wag if we ate at the Kudzu or the Wrangler
Steak House. He wants to take me to the Pink House on the
square in Savannah…*

Who was 'R', Starr wondered. Maybe her mom talking
to this guy was all very innocent, but Starr's stomach was
turning over again much as the day before and she tried
to quell the burning that began to surge in her arteries.
She read on:

*I had a wonderful time with R tonight. He's got a great
sense of humor and for someone with his physique, he has the
gentlest of touch.*

R was touching her mom?

*He brought me home after dinner and came inside.
I know the busybody, Mrs. Baker, saw us pull in. But he
respected that and waited until we were inside to kiss me.
The kiss was hot and sweet and I felt something with him I
hadn't felt in years…*

Starr was now beyond sickened at what she read; she
became angry. Livid. "You'd better not have gone to bed
with him," she said aloud.

*…he left after a few minutes. I did want him, but I guess
he was afraid of doing it with the wife of a man who was*

fighting for his country in Vietnam. And he did mention a couple of days ago that he respected Blake's decision to go. But he also said Blake was stupid for leaving someone as beautiful as me behind.

Starr slammed the diary shut once again and decided that was all she needed for the morning. She was also afraid to read further, as though she somehow knew what her mother was about to do with this R person. She swung her legs off the sofa and went up to her room to talk with Mr. Garcia. He was putting the finishing touches of stain on the ceiling trim.

"Miss Starr, we'll be done here in a few minutes. Did you find out what the book was about that I found?"

"It was just someone's diary. Nothing important."

"I just wondered. Sometimes people find very valuable things that have been hidden away for many years. One of my carpenters discovered a painting last year between the walls of a house and the homeowner told us later it was painted by a famous French artist over two hundred years ago. Was your diary that old?"

"No. Probably ten years ago. Like I said, it doesn't amount to anything."

But it did. It contained the innermost thoughts and feelings of a woman, unhappy with her marriage and apparently wanting to begin a new relationship with someone other than her husband. Starr would wait until Mr. Garcia left so that she would be alone in the quiet house before opening her mother's journal again. She had mixed emotions about continuing her read. She dreaded finding out yet another thing about her mother that would disappoint her. But as she remained both curious and intrigued, she had to go on.

I got a batch of letters from Blake. I'll go two weeks and not hear from him; then I'll get two or three letters at one time. He says he misses us both and hates that we had our tiffs along the way about the Army and Vietnam. I know he's my husband and the father of our little girl, but I just don't know how I feel about him. Maybe I loved him once for a few weeks, if that's possible to do, but we have been so distant. Actually, I would like to see him come home soon so that we could talk face-to-face rather than through letters and I could really determine once and for all if we are right for one another.

Luann rambled on a bit, again about Starr's cute antics, and she was sure Starr had said the words, 'mama' and 'bobble' for bottle. Her mother had called from Chicago to check on her and the baby. She was planning to visit when school was out and the faculty was dismissed from the junior high school for the summer. After reading a few more pages of mundane written dialogue, Starr sat up straight and caught a quickened breath spawned by her extra heartbeat. There was the mysterious R again.

I went to the fair with R in Richmond Hill last night. We bumped into two couples from Pine River, one of who were the Marshalls, old friends of the Ravenels. Did I ever get a dirty look. But R was so funny and even adorable when it came to Starr. It was like she was his own child. He picked her up and swung her around, laughed with her, kissed her, and even won her a Raggedy Ann doll at the shooting gallery...

The diary slipped from Starr's hands and she sat nearly catatonic for several moments, eyes widened and mouth agape. This was all too freaky. She closed her eyes to fully capture what she had read. It was enough to absorb the part about R acting like her father, which in itself caused her chest to blow up like an over-inflated bicycle tire, but coincidentally seeing the words *Raggedy Ann doll* considering the fact that these dolls were found on Marcie Rose and the other women...It was all *too* freaky. Her heart and stomach couldn't take any more surprises, so she wouldn't read any more today. Tonight she would contemplate the day's revelations from her window seat and look for her star. Her eyes hadn't been up there in weeks.

Starr had missed the night sky. It was a place of solace and comfort for her. The stars were silent, but still spoke to her in a million ancient tongues. They were alive in their twinkling glory, unceasing in brightness and unfailing in trust. They were the diamonds on Heaven's gate. She depended on them to lift her up when she was sad and to fill her void when alone. They would not disappoint her tonight.

"Who is this again?" Blake asked.

"Lyman Carpenter, Detective First Class, Las Vegas P.D."

"Right. What can I do for you, detective?" Blake then laid aside his half-eaten ham sandwich.

"Been reading on the wire about the murders out your way. I just wanted you to know, a young woman out here got her throat cut the same way six or seven years ago."

"Okay." Blake didn't see the immediate relevance, considering the vast number of murders committed each year across the country where young women were the victims.

"Our victim was a red-head also."

"Uh huh. How is that significant to us here?"

"We found a Raggedy Ann doll lying next to her."

Blake sat up quickly in his chair. Now he *was* intrigued.

"And another thing. Not long after our murder here, I was contacted by the San Francisco Police that a body of a red-headed woman turned up out there near the Presidio; and I'll give you just one guess what they found on *her*."

"Another doll."

"Yep. Same M.O. just like yours. So you didn't know about this?"

"No, I didn't," replied Blake.

"It's a wonder the FBI didn't connect these murders by now."

"Yes. Interesting." Blake made the same observation. "Detective, was anyone apprehended for either murder?"

"Unfortunately, no real suspects and no arrests. Both cases are deader than four o'clock."

"Too bad. Can you fax me pertinent information from your file on this murder?"

"Sure. And will you reciprocate?"

"Absolutely."

After their conversation ended, Blake mulled over the fact that apparently there was no two-way street on information when it came to the Bureau. He also wondered if Lanham at the GBI had the information about the California and Nevada murders.

Blake leafed through his Rolodex and pulled out Agent Nelson's card. A moment later, he was on the line. "We did know about it, Blake. But before we connected the East and West Coast dots, we wanted to continue fully analyzing all the similarities and then lay out the information to everyone in the Task Force at one time. We're about to that point now. There were similarities, and there were minor differences as well. But…we think we are putting together a pretty good profile."

"And that would be…?"

"Give me a few more days and we'll pull everyone together here in Savannah to talk about it."

Blake was not very happy about being kept out of the loop. But considering past dealings with both the federal and state Bureaus, this was status quo. Town yokels got to know things whenever big cheese cops thought they had a *need* to know.

CHAPTER TEN

Starr decided she would go to the Kudzu for breakfast with her dad the next morning. Rarely did she have more than a bowl of cereal or a Pop Tart at home, whether it was a school day, a Saturday, or a mid-summer's vacation day.

"*This* is a surprise. What are you hungry for? Some eggs and grits or something?"

"Yuk. No way. I'm in the mood for a chocolate donut."

"Well *that's* healthy."

"About as healthy as your eggs and grits," she sassed.

"Okay, then," he said, strapping on his gun belt. "Let's go. But I have to eat and run. If you're not finished when I am, you'll have to find a way home. No walking. You know I don't want you on the street without someone."

"Maybe later Bobby or Linc can swing by on their rounds."

"Fine. Call me when you're ready to leave. Then I want you to go back home for the rest of the day with the door locked."

"You worry like an old woman, Blake."

"What's this 'Blake' stuff? You're getting mighty impudent, kiddo. Stick with 'Dad' if you don't mind."

"Right, Pop."

"That's better."

Starr took her time on the donut, but it was intentional. She was waiting for Katie's nine o'clock break.

"Would you sit with me, Katie?"

"Sure, Sweetie. This will be a refreshing change from my usual routine. I don't see you here much." Katie dipped her head and locked eyes with Starr. "I got a feeling you want to talk." She paused. "Woman talk?"

No. Well, sort of."

"Okay. What's on your mind?"

Starr was still picking at crumbs from the donut with her fork. "Did you know my mom?"

Katie looked surprised that Luann was to be the topic of conversation. "Not really. We spoke when we saw one another, but I don't believe we ever had a real conversation." She caught herself and re-thought. "Except once. Actually we talked a couple of minutes in that booth over there. I think she was just fishing."

"Fishing?"

Katie clasped her hands and looked down. "I think she may have felt that your dad still had...you know, feelings for me. She didn't come right out with it, but I could hear it in her voice. She made it a point to tell me how much she and your dad were in love. And of course, *you* came up in the conversation. Her eyes were just filled with so much love when she spoke about you. That was only about a week before she…" Katie stopped short of saying 'was killed.'

Starr knew the words Katie had left out. She nodded in reply. "How did Dad do after mom died?"

"I never could tell. I could see the grief in his eyes, but he never let it out. We talked a little. Small talk, you know, but he wouldn't open up. It was like he went into hiding for a couple of years. I saw him most every day about town, but it wasn't the same Blake I knew in high school. But after that, he started coming around more, although we never really 'dated' again." She made the quotation marks with her fingers. "We didn't do anything together except pair up at the Founder's Day Dance or go to an occasional movie. We did have dinner every once in a while." She took a sip of her coffee, made a face and set it down quickly. "Ugh, Cold."

"So, you and Dad didn't get involved again."

"No. He pretty much kept his distance in that department. We had a couple of quick kisses on New Year's Eve and a peck on the cheek after dinner, but that was it. He always just held back, like he wanted us to be platonic. You know, like friends not lovers."

"Were you lovers before?"

"Starr! What a thing to ask. But the answer is 'no.' We

just didn't go that far. Even as close as we were before… your mom. I know one thing: your dad's priority has always been you and nothing or no one will ever get in the way of that. The other night when you all were over for dinner. It was the first time since we were teens that he kissed me like that."

Katie smiled sheepishly when that came out and Starr thought she saw her blush a little. She smiled back, but gave Katie a contemplative stare. "What was my mom like?"

"Pretty. Bright pretty red hair. And very friendly. People even said 'saucy.'"

"Saucy? What does that mean?"

"You know, full of life. Always laughing every time I saw her." Katie paused. "You have her nature, you know. Perky and a little audacious. In a good way, I mean."

Starr's smile faded. "Was she true to my dad when he was in Vietnam?"

Katie's mouth fell open and her eyes widened. "Starr, if you're suggesting your mom…"

"I have to know, Katie. Did you ever see her going around with anyone else?"

" Heavens, no. As far as I know, your mother adored your dad and would never have gone out on him. Why are you asking questions like this?"

"Oh, no reason. Maybe *I* was just fishing, *too*."

"Well, my dear, you're fishing in the wrong pond. Just get any such notions out of your head. I didn't know a whole lot about your mother, but everything I've ever seen or heard about her was nothing but good. She may have liked to have a good time, but she was sweet and loving to your father. There was no one else in her life, I promise you." Katie maintained her look of bewilderment.

"Thanks, Katie. That makes me feel good about her." The swelling began again in Starr's chest as she so passionately wanted to tell Katie about the diary. She needed someone like Katie to bring her mother to life and to personify her words. And words that she had yet to read. How far did Luann Ravenel go with her new interest, the mysterious R?

Shortly after Katie resumed her server duties, Bobby came by the diner for coffee. Before he could sit down, Starr asked him to take her home.

They walked from the diner to the car. "What's up with you today? A kid on summer break should still be sleeping in."

"I never sleep in, school or not. Always stuff to do," Starr replied, sliding onto the front passenger's seat.

"Like what?"

"Detective work. You know, finding killers and such."

Bobby looked puzzled. "You mean in the Jersey murders? I thought your dad put that one to bed."

"It's not all that settled with me. But I'm talking about Marcie Rose's and the others' killer."

"The killer's locked up, Starbright."

"If you mean Jake, he's not the killer. I overheard

Daddy say he didn't do it. And he's got a good nose about people."

Bobby buckled up. "And just who do *you* think the killer is, Nancy Drew?"

"I'm not saying. Don't have it all sorted out, but I will."

"Well when you do solve the case, how about lettin' us poor slobs on the force in on it?" He smiled and dropped the gearshift down into 'drive.'

"But of course. Can I hit the siren?" she asked, snapping her seatbelt.

"Nope. Against regulations unless there's an emergency. So, why aren't you zipping around on your bike these days?"

"Oh, it's Dad. He's afraid I'll be abducted by Rag Doll Man."

"Not likely. He's in jail, remember? And even if he by chance is still out there, what would he want with a little snot like you?"

"I know, I know. I'm a kid and he kills older people. I went through this with my dad a couple of times."

Bobby looked straight ahead, intending to dodge further dialogue about the subject. "Listen to your dad, Starbright. It can be more dangerous than you think on these streets, small town or not." As he straightened out the corner from Main to Barrett, the exhaust roared on the Crown Vic.

Starr ignored the warning, now seemingly more interested in the car. "This thing pretty fast?"

"Four twenty-nine police interceptor. None of these kids' muscle cars around here will out-run it."

"What's the top end?"

Bobby looked at her and grinned. "What do you want to know that for?"

"Just do, that's all."

"I don't know, probably one fifty to one sixty. Hell, maybe even more."

Starr smiled. She loved speed, although she had only been in the Blazer once when her dad went over seventy-five to over-take a speeder at the edge of town.

"What kind of car do you have, Bobby?"

"You're sittin' in it. The town lets me have the car for personal use. I don't need anything else."

"I think I'd still have my own car if I were a town cop. Maybe a Ferrari or a Corvette."

"On a cop's salary? Right."

When Bobby's squad car left the driveway, Starr went to the fridge, took out a Coke, and settled onto the couch with her mom's diary and a bag of *Lay's*. She stared for more than a minute at the diary in her lap. It screamed to be opened as though the ghost of Luann Ravenel needed to communicate with her daughter. The diary had been stowed away for probably more than ten years and now that it had been found and partially read, Luann's whole story had to come out. Diaries were meant to be personal, but they were also intended to be discovered long after their authors were gone. That those who remained would then know the real them. Diaries made their authors ageless and immortal, and whether in life they could not or chose not for their innermost thoughts to be found out, it would no longer matter when they were dead.

There was still half the diary to go. At last Luann's only child could know her. Really know her.

Before Starr opened the journal to the point where she had stopped reading the day before, she closed her eyes. Was there anything significant about the doll? Was it not ironic that the same doll with the impish smile was the topic of discussion around town and was at the same time turning up in a decade old diary? Was the diary some kind of omen? Was Starr's Annie somehow connected to the Pine River and Savannah killings? She opened her eyes. Her dad may be right. Maybe she did have too vivid an imagination.

Moistening her index finger, she searched for the page and paragraph where she had left off.

...He took Starr and me home and I invited him in. I offered him a drink, but he said he never puts alcohol in his body. I guess maybe I did know that, but forgot. He's a perfect physical specimen and it goes to figure. God, I don't remember him being so good-looking.

We talked a little and I put on some music, my Rolling Stones album. We sat on the couch and listened for a while. Then he kissed me. It wasn't that 'good night' peck that he gave me the other night; it was long and slow and wet. His cologne was intoxicating and everything about him left me breathless. He pulled me close and I fell into him. We made out for several minutes, then....

"Don't do it, Mom," Starr shouted in her mind. Her heart raced again and she despised where this was going.

...he started unbuttoning my blouse. He ran his hand inside of my bra and touched my nipples. His other hand worked slowly up my thigh and then between my legs. I guess my brain just went numb and I pulled him down on me. Geez, I feel like I'm writing a Harlequin novel and I'm getting aroused again and he's only been gone an hour.

"*We made love in front of the fire. I've never had such a romantic and sexually fulfilling experience as tonight. I do feel somewhat guilty though, but not as much as I thought I would. It's strange. While we were making love, Blake never entered my mind.*

This time, Starr hurled the diary across the room, striking a ceramic lamp on the end table by the recliner. It toppled over and crashed onto the carpet into several pieces. "And I suppose you did 'the nasty' right in front of me!" she said aloud. "How could you, Mom? And how could you do this to Dad? He was probably in some fox hole while you were making it with Raggedy Ann Man."

The words came out accidentally, but as soon as she said them, they kept echoing in her head. *Raggedy Ann Man.* Why would she call him that when she had earlier referred to the killer as Raggedy Ann Man? Maybe she wanted him to be the killer and then she could hate him all the more. But now she hated her mother, too. All the notions and feelings she had acquired about her mom from the photographs and in listening to her dad's account of their early days together had been vacuumed from Starr's head. She felt numb, even paralyzed. The lamp lay broken, the coke spilled and chips scattered and crumbled over the sofa cushions. But she didn't care. The mess was the least of her concerns. She just couldn't void her brain of the image. Her mom and this **R,** writhing on the couch. *This* couch.

Starr jumped off the sofa, retrieved the diary and bounded up to her room. Opening her dresser drawer, she placed the diary beneath her underwear. She could never let her dad find it. He would be crushed. When she closed the drawer, she turned her attention to Annie, still perched against the mirror, smiling now sarcastically.

"And you," Starr said. "I hate you too, Annie. You were supposed to be from my mom, not her….boyfriend. Who was he, Annie? You know. You know, all right…"

At that moment the doorbell rang. Starr trotted back down the stairs and peered through the front door glass. Tommy Lee.

"Hey, Tommy."

"Hey," he answered, brushing past her. "Want to go down to the pond? Got my rod."

"I can't. You know I'm under house arrest for a while."

"Yeah, but figured as long as I'm with you your dad would let you go out. Hey, what happened here?" He took account of the lamp, coke bottle and potato chips. "Left over from the tornado?"

"It's nothing. Just had one of my fits, that's all. Help me clean it up."

"What about? Your dad make you mad?" he asked, picking up the drained coke bottle.

"No, my mom..." Starr stopped short, not meaning to say that. She continued meticulously picking the ceramic fragments out of the carpet.

"Your mom? What do you mean? Your mom's...you know...dead."

"I can't go into it, Tommy Lee. Forget what I said."

After the coke stain was dabbed up, Starr ran the vacuum over the couch and carpet. When the mess was fully addressed, the two went up to her room. She automatically sat down at her chess board.

Tommy was not about to let the 'mom' statement go. "So how could you be mad at your mom?"

"It's personal, Tommy Lee. Let it go at that."

"Personal how?"

"You don't give up, do you?"

"Well, I thought we were good enough friends to where you'd tell me why you trashed your living room... because you're mad at a woman who's not living anymore."

Starr sighed, partly from being irritated at Tommy's persistence and partly because she knew she needed to unburden some of this, even at the expense of telling a dumb boy. She would be a great more comfortable sharing her thoughts and burdens with another girl, but she was not that close to any of the girls in town or at school.

"If I tell you something, will you swear you'll never tell another soul? Not even your mom?"

Tommy read the compelling look in her eyes. "Cross my throat and hope to choke."

"You'd better or I *will* hurt you. Bad!"

Tommy Lee nodded emphatically.

Starr looked away toward the dresser and Raggedy Ann for a moment and then began a slow paraphrasing of only selected segments of her mom's diary. Tommy sat listening, emotionless but obviously intrigued. It took her nearly fifteen minutes to recount what amounted to about six months worth of information. She led Tommy up to the point where her mother had sex with *R* the night of the county fair, but intentionally left that information out. She only told him the man came around a few times and they started going out. And *he's* the one that gave her the doll.

When she appeared to be finished and sitting solemnly with her legs characteristically crossed up under her, Tommy asked, "Freaky about the Raggedy Ann. Do you have any idea who this *R* guy is?"

"No. He could be the 'rag doll' killer for all I know."

"Holy crap, I never thought about that. I just figured the doll thing was some kind of coincidence. Can I read it? The diary?"

"No," she replied abruptly.

"You gonna tell your dad about this?"

"No way. It would hurt him. He needs to keep mom in his heart the way he remembers her."

"Maybe he found out about the guy when he got back from the war."

Starr shook her head. "I wouldn't think so."

"Well, you haven't finished reading, so maybe you'll find out who he is at the end. This is like a mystery novel. It could have a surprise ending."

"I've told you enough. Let's talk about something else."

"How about monster man?"

"Kolb?"

"Yeah."

"Dad had him at the station, got his fingerprints and sent them to the GBI. When the Jersey police ran them, they said Kolb wasn't their man."

"Hmm," replied Tommy. "So he's just a weird dude and that's it, huh?"

"Could be. All right, enough talk. Set 'em up," Starr said, placing her pieces on the board.

What Tommy Lee had said did give her hope for a salvageable outcome to the diary. Could her mom ever redeem herself? Did she ultimately reveal Mr. R? Did her dad ever find out about the affair? The suspense began to gnaw. As soon as her dad went to bed, Starr would break out the diary again. She couldn't wait until tomorrow for another installment, painful as it was.

CHAPTER ELEVEN

After supper, Starr returned to her room and pulled her mother's photographs from the foot locker. Luann Ravenel smiled back at her an innocent smile in one photo and then there was that adoring smile she had cast in Blake's direction at their wedding in another. And then there was that smile of love and pride as she held the baby Starr. In a photo with a date stamped on its white edge, October 5, 1972, she was smiling again. Luann was in her bedroom, sitting on the bed's edge. It was the same headboard as her dad's bed. Funny, but Starr never noticed that on the pillow behind her mom was a protruding arm and leg of her Annie. The county fair was always the last of September and the photo would have been taken or developed a week or so later. The smile was for the person taking the picture. Was it R? Starr always loved her mom's smile in that photo. Now knowing who it was probably for, she suddenly hated it.

"What are you doing?" Blake's voice shattered Starr's concentration, startling her.

"What? Oh, nothing. Just looking at mom's old photos."

Blake dropped down and sat cross-legged beside her on the floor. "She was pretty, wasn't she? What prompted you to dig these out tonight?"

"I was just thinking and wondering about her, that's all. I pull this stuff out once a month or so. It helps me imagine what mom was like."

Blake nodded. He gazed nostalgically at his wife's face. "I think that's the last one we ever had of her," he said, pointing at the bedroom photo.

Starr then pointed out the partially hidden doll behind her. "See, there's Annie."

"Yeah, your mom got that for you when I was in Vietnam. Says she got it at the County Fair that year." He smiled.

Starr's heart began to ache when he said that. Poor Dad. Poor naïve Dad, she thought. "Well," she brisked. "I'll put these away and come back down to watch M*A*S*H with you."

"Okay. How does a bowl of butter brickle with it sound? I picked some up at the store on the way home."

"Yeah," she replied gleefully. Her favorite.

"By the way," he added, stopping and turning. "What happened to the table lamp downstairs? I sat down to read the paper and reached to turn on the light and no lamp."

"Just an accident, Dad. I was cleaning and knocked it over," she lied. "It broke. Sorry."

"Well, be more careful next time."

The lights went out in Blake's room just after eleven and when Starr heard no further sounds, she retired to her window seat with the diary and pushed out the windows. For a while she sat scanning the dim stars throughout the humid night sky. It was not a good telescope night. She then looked down at the Kolb house. The light from his kitchen window radiated onto the back deck. Otherwise there was no sign of activity. One day she would like to get a look inside and maybe that would give her a clue as to who Rupert Kolb was and what he was all about.

Starr threw on her pajamas and switched on the lamp by her bed. Returning to her dresser, she pulled out the diary from beneath her underwear and plopped onto the bed.

November 3rd.

I was sick this morning. Couldn't even keep down dry toast. And then it hit me. I'm late on my period. God. I can't be pregnant. I haven't been on the pill since Blake's been gone, but I never dreamed I'd be having sex with another man, either. Made doctor's appointment today in Savannah at an OB/GYN clinic.

November 5th.

Threw up twice this morning. I just don't feel like writing today.

November 11th.

Now I am sick. Dr. Hanary confirmed I'm pregnant. I can't handle this. Need to talk to R. It didn't take me ten minutes to decide what to do. No way I can have this baby. Not only would my marriage be over, but I'd definitely have to leave town. I'd probably be run out of town."

Starr's hands began to tremble as a thousand emotions came over her. But it was the anger and heartsickness that dominated. It was a double whammy. The mother she loved and idolized in picture and story was not only pregnant with another man's baby, but she was going to give it up. It all made Starr want to stop reading for the night even though she had read just a few lines. But she forged on.

R was by again tonight. I couldn't tell him what was going on with me. He did sense something was wrong as he asked me why I was so distant. I guess when two people are having a great time together three or four nights a week for nearly two months and then one of us puts the brakes on, the other will be suspicious. He asked me if I was seeing someone else. I told him no, that I feel like I have a virus. It will come out eventually, so I might as well break it to him. Maybe tomorrow.

November 16th.

I told him tonight. At first he looked stunned. Then he gave me a surprise. He said he guessed we'd have to go ahead and just leave town with Starr and start a new life. Of course that meant beginning divorce proceedings right away. I told him I couldn't do that to a man risking his life in a combat zone whether I loved him or not. When I told R the best thing for everybody was to get an abortion, he flipped totally out. I actually got scared. He got in my face and said no woman is going to kill a baby that belonged to him. I told him it was my decision and he said he would be god damned if it was. He did calm down and then got real moody. After a while he left. He knows I'm dead set on doing this. I'm making an appointment first thing in the morning.

I'm set for the 25th. The clinic had a cancellation. I wish it were tomorrow. Now I not only have to think about it for over a week, but I've got to contend with R. He will have more to say about this for sure.

November 21st.

Just as I thought, R called me up and pleaded with me to stop the abortion. He would go ahead and quit his job, set us up in Savannah or Charleston and get married the day after my divorce. I can't believe him. He seemed like a perfectly sensible guy when we first got together. Now he's---weird. I'm going to tell him we're over. I don't know how he'll react. I've seen a very scary side of him.

R cornered me at the Piggly Wiggly this morning and pulled me off to the side near the bakery. He wanted to know my decision and I told him to call me tonight. He had hold of my arm and said 'no, now.' Then I told him I was going through with it. I thought he was going to hit me. After a minute of staring me down, he walked away without saying anything.

November 25th.

It's done. Got a lot of emotions tonight. I feel so guilty, yet I have a sense of relief. Can't help thinking what it would have been. Feel very sad right now. I cried all day. The phone has kept ringing and I know it's R. Just couldn't take him tonight. God, I think my hormones are all messed up.

November 26th.

R came by to see me. I didn't want him to cause a scene at my front door, so I let him in. I expected him to be mad out of control, but he wasn't. He was actually tender. He sat with me on the couch and held me. I broke down again and he pulled me into him even tighter. We sat for over an hour in one place without saying a word. His tenderness was unexpected, but I loved it. It made the horrible things he said go away. I guess in hindsight, I can understand how he felt. After all, it was his child, too.

Starr slowly closed the diary and let it slip to the floor. For a while she lay still, staring blankly at the cartoon face of her doll on the dresser. All this was actually too much for her heart to digest. After a few moments, she reached over and turned out the light. She sobbed quietly for over fifteen minutes until sleep finally overtook her.

At the breakfast table the next morning Blake noticed Starr's red, swollen eyes. "You been crying, Sweetheart?"

She knew the eyes would give her away as they had

stared pitifully back at her in the bathroom mirror earlier. It wouldn't do to lie.

"Yeah, I guess."

"What's wrong? You're not sick or anything are you?"

"No. Probably just one of those hormonal things." About that, she did lie.

"I don't pretend to know everything about women issues, but I do know you're too young to have hormone things going on."

"Katie said it could happen easily this early in a woman's life."

"Well, in the first place, you're not a woman yet; I know *that* much. And are you talking woman talk to Katie these days?"

"No. But we do talk some these days. I feel good talking to her. She listens good."

"Well," Blake corrected.

"Well what?"

"She listens *well*. I wasn't good at many subjects in school, but I was good in English and Composition. Anyway, is anything troubling you?"

"Nope." Again another lie. She couldn't remember when she had been so troubled. "But guess I've been thinking about Marcie Rose some. I miss her, Dad."

"Yeah, I know you do." He raked his spoon thoughtfully through his *Wheaties*. "I should go by and check on Coach today. Haven't seen him around town in a week."

The journey through her mother's diary was taking an emotional toll on Starr. She had been cross and moody for three days, not to mention sad and tearful. And she didn't know whether to feel sorrier for her dad or herself. As long as she had been aware that her mother existed and had grown to love her through the photos and stories, in her mind Starr had placed her mom in some kind of fantasy shrine. But the woman on the bed in the October photo no longer wore the face of a faithful, loving wife; instead it was the face of an adulteress in the process of throwing away her marriage. There was also the issue of the baby that was never born. A little brother or sister. But her mother had thrown that away as well.

When her dad left for the station, Starr put away the cereal and placed the bowls and utensils in the dish washer. She whiled away nearly an hour cleaning the kitchen and straightening up her dad's room, burning up time that could be spent finishing the diary. It was intentional.

By nine, however, she was curled up on the sofa again affixing her tired eyes onto her mother's words.

Luann had spent the better part of the week following her abortion in Savannah. She had taken a leave of absence from the telephone company since she was out of vacation, pulled Starr from her day care, and took a sabbatical at her dad's house.

December 6th.

I came home today. R knew I'd be here sometime this afternoon, but I didn't tell him when. I found him waiting on the street in his car. He told me he had been there over an hour.

He got me really upset today. He started badgering me again about getting a divorce and leaving town with him. Says he loves me and won't take 'no' for an answer. He wants us to go before Christmas and spend the holidays in Cancun or the Bahamas. I told him I just couldn't do that and since Blake would be coming home soon, it was a good time for Starr and me to get reacquainted with him. He said he knew I didn't love Blake, so why should I be in a nothing marriage. I never said I didn't love Blake. We may not have had much, but maybe we could get something back.

R was livid. He told me in his words 'that's not going to happen.' Actually, he gave me some type of ultimatum. Either leave with him or there would be consequences. I asked him what he meant by 'consequences.' He said he didn't mean that as a threat, but I know he did. I can't believe he said these things. Only a couple of months ago, he was so loving and gentle. It's like he's a completely different personality---obsessed, I guess is the word for it. So angry and threatening.

On the way out the door he gave me a long kiss. Funny. It was like I felt nothing. Maybe I was just tired. Maybe he just pissed me off to a point where he killed any feeling I had for him. He says he'll call me tomorrow. If he brings up the subject of leaving with him again, I won't talk to him at all.

I can't believe it. I had just written the last line and he called. It's 10:30 for God's sake. He also woke up Starr. He had said no more than 'hello' and started on me again. I got really ugly and not proud of the tirade I went into. I finally just told him I'm fed up with his demands and don't want to see him again. I told him I got a letter from Blake (which I did) and he's coming home on the 23rd for Christmas and for good. R started yelling at me and I told him I wasn't going to talk to him again and slammed the phone down.

Luann continued on for several pages, covering about two weeks of inner thoughts and observations. She wrote of the peace of mind she had in not hearing from R. He hadn't called since that stormy night she 'slammed' him out of her life. But it was like waiting for the other shoe to drop. Someone that intense and possessive doesn't give up that easily.

She needed to get 'right' in her head about Blake and try to make a go of it again. Maybe she would feel differently about him this time. After all, he was getting discharged, so at least he'd be around to be a husband to her and father to Starr.

Luann filled up more than thirty pages with her hopes and dreams, plans and designs. But first, she had to void her head of a lot of things: the R affair, her pregnancy, the abortion and not the least of which were the nagging memories of her house-of-cards marriage these two years. Could they really make it? She would damn sure try on her end.

Christmas night.

Blake got home as he said he would on the 23ʳᵈ. When he got off the plane at the Savannah airport, I saw this tall, tanned sergeant that stood out from all the rest. He looked thin and drawn, but I had never seen him look so handsome.

"We stayed in Savannah at the Marriott. Just him and me. Starr stayed with her granddad. I think I was just as hungry for him as he was for me. We made love two, no three times. It was like two whole years were made up in one night. All the ills and hard feelings between us seemed to melt away with every sweet thrust of his body. After we laid there a while, we started talking. I don't know why he said it, but he told me he never messed around on me in Vietnam. And I believe that. But it just made me see myself in the mirror as who I had really become this past year---nothing but an ungrateful, unfaithful_____. Maybe I should just go ahead and write down the word 'whore' and get it over with. I'm just so sorry I strayed.

"But, I don't want to dwell there. I'd rather write about how we spent Christmas today. Starr got a dozen things from Santa, but I really think she liked the Vietnamese doll Blake brought her back. It has shiny black long hair and is dressed in a long, silk thigh long top with slits on the side. She's wearing white silk bottoms. The whole outfit is just darling. If all the women look and dress like this doll, I don't know how Blake managed to resist them. Of course, you don't see too many girls that look like that in a foxhole. Blake just couldn't get enough of Starr today. I

can't remember seeing Mr. Serious laugh so much. He may be a stranger to her, but it didn't take her long to warm up to him. It does seem so ironic that two men have given my Starr dolls in the past six months. Just like this new man in Starr's life, she has now taken to this new little doll. I guess Raggedy Ann will just have to make friends with this little Asian doll. Ha!

Starr laid the journal down in her lap and thought for a bit. She didn't remember any Vietnamese doll. She wondered what happened to it. Did it get lost or destroyed somehow?

I do know one thing. I can't ever let Blake find this diary. It's been my friend and catharsis at times. My very soul lies here in these words. I'm not proud of some things I've divulged to myself. When I go back over what I wrote about being with R, I actually get sick at my stomach. Guess the truth hurts.

I found a place in the attic to hide it. There's a kind of cubby hole with a little door that leads to where people had stored stuff. I'm putting it on top of one of the beams where it's really dark. God help me if anyone ever finds it.

For the first time in three days Starr felt a release from the tightness in her chest. Each time she had opened her mom's diary, she experienced an anticipatory tenseness and as to what more she would discover about her mother. At last, her mom and dad were together again. She wished there were a picture of them together that special Christmas when he came home from the war and made everything right between them; that Christmas when Luann Ravenel did what she needed to do to redeem herself.

Blake cruised slowly down Sydenstricker in the Blazer past Bessie Cotter's house, slowing even more to throw a hand up to the perpetual porch sitter. She nodded in exchange, then spat a stream of brown juice over the banister and onto the red clay. Was she correct about the black Suburban, Blake thought, or did she see anything at all through her distorted living room glass that night?

He reminisced the day he stopped along that same dirt road on his way to Coach's house to flirt innocently with fourteen year old Marcie Rose coming home from school, books cradled into her chest. She paused to strike a playful Hollywood pose, one arm behind her head and eyelashes fluttering. "Well, I do declare, handsome older man," she said in her best Southern drawl. "I believe you're tryin' to pick me up."

"Well, sweet cheeks. You put about ten years and twenty pounds on you and I do believe I'll do just that." He laughed and moved on toward the house.

That was more than four years before. She would have been just a little older than Starr then. As the St. Clair house loomed ahead at the end of the road, his mind almost had him believing she was inside in her bedroom with a couple of girlfriends, dancing to the Go-Go's latest top forty hit, *We Got the Beat*.

Charlie St. Clair heard him pull up and went to the front door. He was now ever vigilant when vehicles came down Sydenstricker. *Now* for Beulah's sake. He waved as Blake pulled up to a stop. Through the windshield Blake saw a man on the porch that looked as if he had aged ten years in two months. He killed the engine and waved back.

It had been two weeks since they saw one another. Coach had not been in town but once in the past month. Blake had not made an effort to come out primarily because he hated so much seeing this tower of a man weeping like a child. He knew that avoiding his mentor like that was being self-minded and weak, and day after day he chastised himself for not going to see him more often.

But the coach seemed to be in better spirits and ready to talk football. It was already August and practice would begin in a week. As they had for the past eight years, the two men contemplated the talent and analyzed each returning player on the squad, one by one. Would Coach have his heart in this season? How would that be possible when his beloved child had been in her grave only a scant two months? His face may have said football, but the winning glint in his eyes was missing.

And then Coach would take note of the cheerleaders on the sidelines at the first game. He would forgetfully look for the sweet face of his daughter mouthing the words to one of their chants. But that face would be missing. How indeed could he get through Pine River High School's first game?

More than two hours later, Blake pulled out of

Sydenstricker onto 41. He shook his head sadly, having serious doubts about whether the Saint would have the mental and emotional stamina to endure the season. But Blake would be there for him, on the side lines, in the locker room, anywhere in Coach's pocket, whenever he was needed.

Starr closed the journal and smiled. Now only a dozen pages were left. Setting the book aside, she went to the kitchen and made herself a peanut butter and jelly sandwich for lunch. Her dad had told her that her mom would rather have a PB & J sandwich than cake or pie. Starr would finish the diary that afternoon. And that night it would be returned to its special hiding place, its home for nearly ten years.

New Years Day.
Blake went hunting this morning with a couple of guys from his high school football team. It let me catch up a little bit here. We went to a New Year's Eve party at Carletta's to listen to this great band, the Allman Brothers, back from their tour. Over in a corner sitting at a table by himself was R. I wonder if he knew we'd be there? I looked in his direction and smiled, but he only sat there and stared at us. It was the coldest, maybe the scariest stare I ever remember seeing. I whisked Blake across the room where we would be out of his sight and no chance Blake could see him. Blake is so perceptive. He would pick up R's stare in an instant. Still through the crowd, I could see him every once in a while

looking at us. It so unnerved me, I faked a headache and told Blake to take me home. We did stay to listen the band's new hit, 'Trouble No More.' It just seemed to fit, considering the last 30 days of crap I went through with R. Blake and I were home by 11:00 and neither of us was awake to see 1973 in.

January 16th.

This was a horrific day for me. For several days I had a feeling when I walked downtown someone was following me. I knew if there was, it had to be R. Today Blake left for Greenville to go to his uncle's funeral. Starr had a high fever and it was cold anyway, so we didn't go. R must have known it as he came by the house wanting to talk to me. I wouldn't let him in, but he barged in anyway. There was a look in his eyes like pure evil. He wanted to know how things were with Blake and if I felt like it was a mistake letting him back into my life. I told him he was never really out of my life. He was just in Vietnam. He reminded me that I told him I wanted to leave Blake and I guess I did tell him that a couple of times. He also asked me if the time and the bed we shared meant anything at all to him. I told him flatly that it was the biggest mistake I had ever made and wanted him to leave. I could see he was upsetting Starr, too. She stood by my leg holding the little Vietnamese doll. Suddenly, he reached down and snatched the doll from her and yelled something like 'So you like this chink doll better than the one I got you, huh?' Then he broke the head and arms off the doll right in front of her. Starr screamed and cried. That was all I could take. I picked up a snow globe that was sitting on the coffee table and hit him with it. It broke and water and fake snow went all over. It cut his head and he drew back like he was going to hit me. He didn't though, but I'll never forget his words. He said 'No one rejects me and gets away with it. Be afraid when you go out, bitch. One day your little darling here might not see you again.'

God, I was chilled. I'm still shaking, but Blake is back and in bed. I feel safe, now. Poor little Starbright. She was so pitiful standing there looking at her broken up doll. I want to tell Blake so he can keep an eye on us, but in telling him, he will know everything about R and me. What can I do? God I've really messed my life up."

Starr's throat swelled nearly shut and large tears rolled down her pink cheeks onto her blouse like heavy raindrops. She felt her mother's fear as sure as if she were experiencing it herself. But after all, she was also there at the ugly scene and perhaps even at two years old, there was enough trauma from that event to stay repressed all these years. So, that's what happened to her doll. The bastard, she thought. And where was he now?

Starr read the last entry. There was only one paragraph.

January 24th.

I went out to the Farmer's Market today and on the way back, I caught sight of R's truck behind me. At first, he got up real close to me and then backed off. I knew he was trying to scare me. Then suddenly he got up on my rear a second time and bumped me. I lost control and spun into a ditch. I thought he was going to get out and hurt me in some way, but he just drove by my car real slow, looking at me and drove off. Someone came by and helped pull me out. Why is R tormenting me like this? Now I'm scared to go out anywhere. Thank God Starr wasn't with me. Blake will be upset about the Mustang. There's a huge dent in the bumper and the front end shakes. I'm just so tired and drained about it all. More tomorrow.

That was the last entry. The diary was like an uncompleted opera. Luann's song was over too soon. But she had given her daughter the words to complete that song. Twelve year old Starr Ravenel, small town streetwise kid, mature as most seventeen year olds, realized that beyond the shadow of any doubt, the man called R had killed her mother. Luann Ravenel did not fall asleep or lose control of the car on her own. She was forced or knocked off the Nine Mile Bridge into Painters Creek. Starr's revelation did not stop there. R was a psychopath and how many psychopaths would there be in a town like Pine River? How many were associated in one way or another with a Raggedy Ann doll? As the ghost of Luann Ravenel had come out of the cubbyhole to point a finger to her murderer, it was up to Starr and no one else to find out who that killer was. Did her mom also fall victim to the man who would later become the Rag Doll Killer?

At supper that evening Starr sat quietly separating beans from corn in her plate, morsel by morsel, as though the process were the meticulous repair of a watch. She had yet to take a bite of anything. Blake eyed her suspiciously for a few moments, then laid down his fork.

"Okay. What gives, Starr? I haven't seen you this quiet in a long time."

She looked up from her plate. "What?"

"That's what I'm asking. What's been going through your mind these past few days? You're like a zombie half the time."

She dropped her eyes to her plate again. "This…may sound a little strange," she stumbled, "but did mom ever mention any of her old boyfriends to you?"

"Why would you ask me something like that?"

"Oh, I'm just always wondering things about her, like who her friends were before you got together, who she hung out with, who she dated. You know, just ordinary things about her. And personal things. Things you may even have forgotten about her. It's just that I have always wanted to put together a complete picture of who she really was. Like pieces in a puzzle. And boyfriends are a part of that picture."

There were lines of concern in Blake's face. "What's got you thinking so much about your mom?"

"I've been *dreaming* about her." That wasn't a lie. She did dream about her mother two nights before. "I just want to know everything you can remember about her, that's all."

"Well, I guess it's natural for a girl going into womanhood to want to know more about her mother. A mother she never knew, except as a baby." He took a sip of water and nodded. "Boyfriends, huh? I don't know. I really don't. She had just moved here shortly before I met her and never really talked about her life in Chicago much. She did date Roy McIntyre before me. Don't know if you knew that. She kind of thought he was a jerk.... possessive, I think she said. Then she broke it off with him and we started going out. That's it for boyfriends. As far as girlfriends? I don't know that she ever got close to anyone. I kind of hoped she would while I was in Vietnam, so she wouldn't be so lonely. Guess she never did."

Except the 'R' creep, whoever he was, thought Starr. Maybe Mr. R was Roy McIntyre.

"Anyway," continued Blake, "we were together less than three years, really two. I was overseas for a year, you know. I swear, I can't remember a whole lot more. It's been almost ten years since she left us. Funny how stuff leaves your mind."

Starr nodded. She guessed that was about as far as she could take her inquisition. It appeared her dad knew nothing about R or anyone else. She decided to change the subject. "So, Father dear, do you plan to get married again?" She smiled, now taking a bite of her cold chicken.

"Maybe. If that special person comes along."

"What about Katie?"

"What about her?"

"Is she that special person?"

"I don't know. Maybe. Maybe not, too."

"I've got a feeling it's 'maybe.' I'd like that, you know."

Blake didn't respond. What was left of his dinner was cold, too. He cleared his setting from the table and chucked the food down the garbage disposal.

He then slapped on his patrol belt and secured the Glock, snapping the hammer strap. "Lock up here good. I've got to make a couple hours worth of rounds and close out the Daily Log at the station. Be back about nine-thirty or ten."

CHAPTER TWELVE

After closing down the station, Blake radioed Bobby who was coming on shift. "Leaving to go home. Did you get some good shut-eye today?"

"Yeah. Except the frigging dog next door kept waking me up with his barking. Tomorrow I'm gonna get 'official' with the owners. Seems to me that knowing a cop lives next to them, they would take extraordinary measures to keep that mutt quiet. Nose to nose tomorrow."

Blake decided to swing by Garden Hills Estates, home to the country club elite, before going home. There were actually no hills in the swanky sub-division; it just sounded like a good, snobbish name to its developer. There had been some vandalism on the golf course on several occasions during the summer and at the special request of the mayor, who happened to *be* one of the elite, the area was canvassed by Blake and his team daily.

At just after nine forty-five Blake signaled a left turn

into Garden Hills from Germantown Road. Pulling from the sub-division across his path was a large black Suburban with black-out glass. Blake stopped and watched as the SUV made a right turn. He could see it was not Kolb's truck as there was a *Support the Arts* bumper sticker on the rear. And a taillight was out. This gave him Probable Cause.

Blake flipped on the blue lights and blew a quick blast on his siren. The driver pulled the Suburban to the curb and stopped almost immediately. Switching to an alternate frequency, Blake radioed the State Patrol. "Pine River to dispatcher, over."

"This is Dispatch. Is that you, Chief Ravenel?" a woman's smoky voice asked.

"Roger. Can you run a tag for me, Ruby?"

"Send it."

"GA tag BA 1349, 1979 or '80 Chevy Suburban."

"Wait one."

In his brights, Blake could see that the lone occupant was a male. He wasn't moving around or reaching for his license. He was stone still. Apparently the vehicle hadn't been running long as there was white vapor from the exhaust drifting across the rear end. This meant the man had either spent the evening visiting someone or sat somewhere for a long time with the engine off.

After a few moments the dispatcher came back to Blake. "The car is registered to Gerald Wayne Bishop, 1451 Mercury Street, Savannah. No warrants and vehicle is not, repeat not stolen."

"Thanks, Ruby." Blake changed back to the Pine River freek. "Bobby, this is Blake. One two eight at Garden Hills and Germantown. Tag # BA 1349."

"You need back-up?" came the reply.

"Not at this time. Will advise. Out."

Blake exited his vehicle and noticed the driver's window on the SUV was still up, engine running and the man was still not moving. When he was even with the left rear wheel, he unsnapped the hammer strap on his holster and rapped his knuckles on the quarter panel. "Sir, please turn off your engine and roll down your window!" he commanded loudly.

When the driver did not respond immediately, Blake slapped the sheet metal again and yelled, "*Now*, please!"

Slowly the window came down and the engine killed.

"Get out of the vehicle and keep your hands where I can see them!"

Again the driver failed to timely respond and Blake formed his fingers around the grip on his Glock. He was about ready to give the man another order when the door opened and the first of two feet planted on the asphalt. Blake tightened his fingers on the gun, then the illuminated face of a white man perhaps fifty two or three came into view. His hands were open, but remained near his side.

"Sir, may I see your license and registration?"

The man reached into his back pocket and produced a wallet from which he took the two documents. "Is there a problem, officer?" he asked. "I wasn't speeding."

Blake didn't answer immediately, but verified from the license photo that the driver was indeed Bishop.

"No, you weren't. I stopped you because your left taillight is out."

"Oh, sorry," Bishop replied.

"You have business here in Pine River, Mr. Bishop? I see you're from Savannah."

Bishop showed some uneasiness with the question, shuffled his feet a little and looked down. "Just visiting a friend. There's no law against that, is there?"

"A friend. Who?"

"I don't think I have to tell you that, sir."

Blake moved closer to the man. "Let me put it to you this way: I stop a man from Savannah who I haven't ever seen in Pine River, coming out of a pricy country club late in the evening. I believe as a law officer responsible for the safety of this town I have a right to ask you that."

"Yes, sir. I understand that. But my reason to be here is personal. And I don't believe I am compelled to tell you what."

Patience with the man was wearing thin. "Please step to the rear of your car and keep your hands in plain sight, sir."

Reluctantly, Bishop did as instructed. Blake brought his flashlight up to the left side of the car and shined its light into the front seat and floor. A few papers were scattered about and a briefcase lay on the passenger side seat. Moving the beam to the back seat, he found it empty; but when he trained the light on the back floor, the hairs on the back of his neck stood up. Across the driveline hump laid the unmistakable red and white striped dress of Raggedy Ann.

Blake pulled his Glock and cocked the hammer. Moving slowly toward the rear of the SUV with the pistol at his side, he grabbed Bishop by his sleeve and spun him into the lift gate. "Spread your feet apart and place your hands on the lid, Mr. Bishop."

"What is the meaning of this?" the man protested. "I've done nothing wrong."

Patting the man down, he found no weapon. "Why is there a doll in your back floor?" As soon as he said the words, he realized how ridiculous he sounded.

"What?" Bishop replied in an astonished tone. "What about it? It belongs to my granddaughter, if you must know."

"I will have to verify that."

"Why? What's the big deal with a doll? Is it against the law in Pine River to have dolls in your car?"

Blake turned Bishop around and allowed the headlights of the Blazer to fully illuminate the man. His eyes looked earnest enough, but antisocial personalities can be deceptively convincing. "Sir, we're looking for a suspect who would have this kind of doll in his possession. That may sound strange, but you need to bear with me while I verify a few things."

Bishop looked down at Blake's right hand. "Can you put that away? It's…making me nervous."

Blake dropped the Glock into its holster. "All right.

Now please take a seat inside of my vehicle." He opened the door for Bishop. "I need to ask you a few more questions."

"Okay, what do you want with me?"

"Mr. Bishop," Blake began, sliding onto the driver's seat beside him. "Now you can help me move this along by answering my first question. Who are you visiting here?"

Bishop stared at Blake a moment, then dropped his head against the seat back and sighed. "Your mayor, Tom McCown." he replied softly.

Blake frowned at the name. "McCown? Are you a friend of his?"

"Yes." Again, barely audible.

"If I call him, will he verify that?"

Bishop turned his head slowly toward Blake and hesitated before answering. "I wish you wouldn't call him, officer."

"And why the hell not?"

"He *is* a friend, you know."

"Yes, you said that," Blake replied.

"It...would be most embarrassing for me to go forward with this conversation. It would be even more embarrassing for the mayor if you called him. Do you know where I'm going with this?"

"Yeah, I get the picture, Mr. Bishop."

Blake began to realize the man was for real. He wouldn't have mentioned Tom McCown's name if in fact he was not his friend or whatever. That would be too easy to check out. He sighed. It would have been all too perfect…the black Suburban, the Savannah stranger, the Raggedy Ann. He would have a genuine suspect. But Blake was again back to square one with a boy behind bars he knew didn't kill Marcie and the other women.

"Get the taillight fixed, sir. I'm letting you off with a warning."

Bishop broadcast his indignation once again with a glare and responded sarcastically, "Thanks. Have just a wonderful night, officer."

Six o'clock came early the next morning. One of these days he would get to sleep in on a Saturday. In a half hour, Blake was showered, poured into a fresh uniform and wolfing down a granola bar. He stopped to leave Starr a note:

> *Call me when you get up. And don't go anywhere till I get home.*
> *Love, Dad.*

Stopping off to have a cup of coffee at the Kudzu with Linc, he slid in the booth opposite the husky deputy.

"Mornin', Chief. Rough night? You look a little piqued today."

"You think so? Maybe I just need a vacation. I think before school starts, I'm gonna take a couple of days with Starr down at Amelia. I told her one day we'd do some fishing. You know, a little father-daughter weekend."

"Good idea. Go for it."

A hulking figure in seersucker with a rolled up newspaper under his arm interrupted. "What are we going *for?*"

Blake turned in his booth. "Mayor. Good morning." An interesting coincidence, he thought.

"Blake. Lincoln. Mind if I join you?" he pulled up a chair perpendicular to the two men before anyone could answer. "What's the status on the Thigpen boy?" He got right to the point.

"He's been charged by the D.A., Tom. That's as far as it's gone. I thought we had a sure thing last night on a potential suspect. I stopped a black Suburban…"

"Are you still chasing your tail on this Suburban theory of yours? If you believe ol' Bessie Cotter about that, then you're as loony as she is, boy."

"As I was saying. I stopped this guy and he fit our profile to a tee. Even had a Raggedy Ann in the back of his SUV."

"Hell," said Linc. "*I'd* have been all over *that* one. And you let him go?"

"Yeah, he was just visiting from Savannah and apparently the rag doll belonged to his granddaughter. His story was verifiable, so I didn't press it."

"Who was he?" the mayor asked.

"His name was Bishop. White haired man in his early fifties."

McCown cleared his throat and shuffled his body in the chair. "Well, I'm sure you did right in trusting your instincts about the man and letting him go, being the thorough policeman that you are. After all, that's why we made you Chief, my boy." He chuckled nervously and glanced at his watch. "Hey, gotta run. The paper chase never lets up." He stood, shook hands with the officers and hurried out the door.

Linc gave Blake a puzzled look. "What was *that* all about? I never saw the man clear out of *any* conversation so fast."

Blake just smiled and finished off his coffee. Katie, who stopped by the table to refill their cups, thought the smile was for her.

Nine forty-five, Saturday.

"Kudzu Diner. This is Katie."

"Hi, Katie. It's Starr."

"Well hi, sweetie. How're you doing? You and Tommy Lee still going to see the new E.T. movie this afternoon?"

"I don't know. Maybe. But listen, can I come over again to see you? We *really* need to talk, now."

"We do? What's going on?"

"I found out something and I just need someone to talk to. It can't be Dad and it's too personal to tell Tommy Lee."

"Sounds serious."

"Pretty much.

"Okay. I take my lunch break at eleven thirty, but I only have a half hour."

"Eleven thirty. I'll be there."

Even though Blake and Katie had danced around any kind of meaningful relationship for more than eight years, that is until recently, Starr and Tommy Lee had been playmates since she was in the fourth grade. It wasn't that Starr liked hanging with boys more than girls or vice versa with Tommy, but they had become friends as a result of a school playground incident. Tommy had come to Starr's rescue when another fourth grader, a boy who learned early on from his hostile father the ways of a bully, pushed her down. Not that Starr wasn't feisty enough to take her own part, but Tommy had also been pushed around by the larger boy the day before and saw an opportunity in Starr's incident to redeem his pride. As the bully stood over the fallen Starr, hands on hip, taunting her, Tommy ran from behind and with the blitzing speed of an offensive guard, bowled the kid over. It stunned the boy and after he hit the turf, Tommy bounded onto him, fists poised to strike. Unfortunately for Tommy, a teacher happened by at the very time Tommy knocked the bully down. Tommy was suspended for two days, but the good news was that the bully never harassed another kid.

When Tommy returned to school, a grateful Starr came up to him and said, "Thanks for taking up for me and sorry it got you suspended. But I could've taken him by myself, you know."

Although Tommy was a year behind in age and school and there were certainly gender differences, a friendship was struck. Nearly every weekend for the past three years Starr was either at Tommy Lee's house or he at hers.

She taught him the skill of chess and he taught her important things like how to line up her thumbs and blow into a wide blade of grass to make a whistle and the proper way to filet bloodworms for the hook.

Along the way, Starr and Katie became close as well. Katie was gradually becoming her unofficial surrogate mother. As Starr continued to mature emotionally, physically and intellectually, there was more and more 'woman talk.' She needed Katie. She needed an adult female with which to share personal things. And when she and her dad had the occasional fight, Katie was the one who took up for her. Katie was referee, counselor and mother-figure all rolled into one.

They sat in a booth near the entrance to the kitchen to give them a little more privacy. Although Katie had suggested they have lunch on one of the outside benches at the Tastee-Freeze, she then realized that by the time she drove them out and back, much of her lunch break would be over. Anyway, it was just too stinking hot to sit outside.

"Did your dad drop you off here?"

"No, I biked."

"You know he'll be upset about that. He just doesn't want you out running around with all that's going on. We could've talked later at home, you know."

"Yeah, but I couldn't wait another hour, Katie. I have

to get all this out of my system now. And being cooped up in the house all day long…I just can't stand it any longer. I feel like I've been under house arrest for two months. At least Dad is letting me go to the movies this afternoon."

Katie gave her an understanding nod and took a small bite of her grilled cheese sandwich. "Is this a 'woman' thing you want to talk about? Have you been paid your first visit by the old maid?"

Starr squinched up her nose. "What are you talking about?" Then the light bulb came on. "Oh. No. No, not yet. I'm sure that's just around the corner, seeing that I'm already a woman."

Katie stifled a smile. "Okay, kiddo, then what's bothering you? I knew there was something on your heart the other day when we talked. I have a feeling you were more than just curious about your mom. Is this still about her?" Katie was indeed a perceptive person. Waitresses are like hairdressers and bartenders. All are in position to take on other people's problems; most have empathic ears and eventually a great many become lay therapists.

For Starr to initiate a discussion about her mother's diary was like trying to crank a car with a weak battery on a cold morning. She was not at all too sure she was doing the right thing in parlaying the private thoughts of another, most of all about her own mother; but if there was anyone she could tell, it was Katie. After stammering and hem-hawing a bit, she took a deep breath and said "Okay, here goes."

She told Katie about Luann's anger when Blake

decided to join the Army which planted him a year later in the jungle of Vietnam. Nothing out of the ordinary there. Then she painfully told her about the mysterious stranger, R, with whom she had a two month long, sordid affair. That stopped Katie in mid-bite. Starr told of how Luann ended the relationship, the man's angry response and how she grew fearful of him. And then she told how her mom and dad reconstituted their marriage after he returned home. Katie sat wide-eyed and fully intrigued. Now she knew why Starr was so bent on finding out more things about her mother. Starr needed reinforcement and peace of mind about her so that she could regain the admiration and respect that she had acquired over the years from hearing nothing but good things about her.

But Starr was not through. There was her suspicion that her mom's obsessed lover had something to do with her death, perhaps even forcing her off the bridge. After all, he had already bumped her off the road. And there was the mystery of the doll. Was it too much of a coincidence that Raggedy Ann was a significant player in two tragic but different scenarios? Was there somehow a connection?

Starr had bent Katie's ear for an hour. Katie had remained silent and stoic. Mostly she was just stunned with it all. As it was now after 12:30, dragon lady, Minnie Ruthouse, had already complained to the owner that Katie had abused her lunch break and it had been long since time to take hers.

"Starr, dear," said Katie swinging her legs out from the booth. "We *do* need to talk more about this. Go on home before your dad finds out you were here. Maybe you can come by tonight, okay?"

When they broke up, Starr walked past the booth directly behind where she had been sitting. It had been occupied the past hour by Irma Beasley who sat nodding and smiling to herself. She, by the way, had the biggest ears in town and a tongue longer than a snake plant. And she couldn't wait to wag it. It was her job, after all, and she relished sharing *any* lip-sucking piece of gossip.

The story hit the town immediately like the mid-summer tornado that had rocketed through the month before. As the storm damage was pretty much repaired in the last thirty days, the damage done to the Ravenels by the mouth of a little old lady with white hair, green eyes and the bluest blood in the county, may be irreparable. By four o'clock no less than a hundred people in Pine River knew that Starr had found her mother's diary and uncovered not only the story of Luann's affair, but quite possibly the identity of her mother's and Marcie Rose's killer.

Blake had been tied up in a meeting with the mayor and town council for two hours, else he would've heard the gossip earlier. But when he returned to the station, it was Anna Mae who broke the news to him. "And I could just slap Irma Beasley three ways from Sunday for spreadin' that story. Does the woman have no shame? She's got all that money, so why does she have to draw attention to herself by spreadin' manure all over town?"

Blake felt like he had just been kicked in the gut. Linc and Bobby had nothing to say, but couldn't help staring at him with their 'deer in the headlight' look. There was only emptiness and embarrassment on Blake's face and his wounded eyes said it all. "Excuse me, fellows. I need to get home."

When the first call had come into the house around three from one of Starr's schoolmates, Jenny Bradford, it caught Starr off guard. And when she learned from Jenny that the word had gotten around about the diary and who may have committed the murders, Starr was aghast. How did that happen? Had the unthinkable occurred? Did Katie blab? She couldn't have. She wouldn't have even let it slip out accidentally. The second call *was* from Katie. "I'm sorry, sweetheart. Your voice must've carried more than we thought and right into the ear of Old Mrs. Beasley. I've tried calling your dad, but he isn't in."

After that, the minister called, wanting to talk to her dad. She knew what about. And Tommy called. "Geez, Starr. You didn't tell me all the stuff that was in that diary. The word around is that you know from the diary who may have killed Marcie and those women."

"I didn't say that. I have no idea who the killer is. I was just speculating because of the doll. God, I won't be able to show my face to anybody. Now everybody will think bad things about my mom. And dad will really be hurt over this. I could crawl in a hole and die."

She heard the key turning the lock in the front door. Because her dad was home at four-thirty, a full two hours earlier than normal, Starr knew the word had gotten to him. She sat in the living sofa chair, balled up into a tiny form and eyes puppy-dog forlorn. At first he didn't say a word; no "Hey, Starbright. How was your day" like usual. His eyes only made casual contact with hers while he took off his pistol belt and sat quietly, slowly down on the sofa opposite her. He said nothing for a full minute, but stared off through the living room window and beyond that perhaps into another world. A world ten years before.

"When were you planning to tell me about this?" he finally asked in a soft, almost inaudible voice.

Starr's lower lip quivered. "Guess you heard, huh?"

"What in God's name were you thinking, Starr?"

She didn't answer.

"Why would you go to that diner and talk to Katie about the contents of some diary that belonged to your mother? Do you not realize the impact of all this?"

"I didn't think anyone could hear us talking. We were kind of in the back of the diner."

Blake folded his hands under his chin and kept his eyes on hers. "Why couldn't you come to me about this… this diary? Did you think I'd be angry for some reason?"

"There were some things in there that I thought would hurt you, Dad. I didn't want that to happen."

"Don't you think my finding out about it this way hurts even more?"

"I just didn't think that anyone would be eavesdropping.

Guess I didn't think at all. But I had to talk to *somebody* about it, Dad. I was just upset about all that stuff."

"I'm not sure what all *that stuff* is, Starr. All I heard was that you have a diary which mentions a man in your mother's life when I was in Vietnam. That she had an affair with him, she got pregnant and he ended up trying to kill her. And maybe did. And the talk is that you deduced who it was and he could be the killer that we or at least I am looking for. Did I get it all in there?"

"Yes, pretty much," she replied softly.

Blake shook his head and partially covered his face with his hand. He was quiet for a long time. It seemed like five minutes to Starr.

"Give it to me."

"What?"

"*You* know what. The *diary.*"

"I don't want you to read it, Dad."

"Never mind what you do or don't want. Go get it now."

Starr moved slowly off the chair and climbed the stairs to her room. Blake heard what sounded like the closing of a small door overhead and in a couple of minutes she was back with the diary in hand.

He placed the journal onto the end table where there was no longer a lamp and patted the cushion beside him. "Come sit down."

She sat down on the middle cushion and folded her hands gracefully in her lap. Blake put his hand on her head and drew her into his shoulder. "If what is in this book is in any way close to what I've heard, I'm sorry you ended up reading it. It has to hurt and selfishly, I really haven't thought much about *your* feelings."

Starr nodded and then began to cry. It was a reach down deep cry. Her tears practically soaked the left upper side of her dad's shirt near his badge. But it was okay with Blake for the shirt to serve as her handkerchief. They sat without word until the evening sun began to peer into the window, spreading its golden brilliance onto their faces.

The phone startled them. Blake released his arm from Starr's shoulder and got up to answer it. It was Katie. His lowered voice was almost inaudible to Starr. She did hear him say "she's doing all right" and something about seeing Katie tomorrow and they would talk. A couple of minutes later he came back to the couch. "I'll fix supper. Guess it'll be pot luck tonight."

About seven-thirty Starr took her bath and positioned herself as on most evenings in the window seat by her telescope. Over the rooftops and pines the upper winds feathered the thin clouds against a vivid orange-red sky. It would be another beautiful day tomorrow. But in the streets of Pine River, tomorrow would also be another day of gossip and speculation. And for the first day in a long time or perhaps ever, Starr had no desire to be out on those streets.

Blake went to his bedroom with the diary and a bottle of Merlot and closed the door. After lumbering into his wingback chair sitting cattycornered to his bed, he poured the first glass of wine. Opening the cover to the first page, he immediately recognized the penmanship, even after ten years. It never entered his mind that he would ever spend one more night with Luann. Yet what she had written was never *meant* for him to read.

At just before two-thirty Blake had digested the entire diary… the last three years of his dead wife's life. He did not know whether to be angry or sad. He was actually a lot of both. His wife had been unfaithful to him and it did hurt. Another man at least for two or so months had been in his bed. Even worse, the man had designs on being Starr's new father. A dozen questions ran through Blake's brain. Who *was* the man and was he someone who was still around town? Was there any significance to him giving Starr the rag doll? Blake knew the man was angry about Luann's decision to purge him from her life and he was damn jealous about the Vietnamese doll taking the place of Raggedy Ann. And he was a man who obviously revealed psychotic, antisocial tendencies.

Blake pulled a writing pad and pen from the drawer. After jotting down words and phrases like *young, athletic, bought Starr a rag doll, possessive nature, angry* and so on, his head started to spin. Maybe it was the nearly empty bottle of wine that was affecting him. Or perhaps it was all the questions he had in his head. But it was two-thirty in the morning and the long nightmare of a day refused to end. Then he thought about something he read. Leafing back through the pages toward the beginning he re-read: *Latching onto Blake also got me away from someone*

I thought was a creep and obsessed with me, but who I later found so different.

Blake looked up from the journal and brought a clinched fist down on the arm of his chair. Roy. Roy McIntyre. Was he the R man? Did Luann take back up with him? Blake knew she thought Roy was a creep and was certainly obsessed with her. And that was one reason she dumped him. He was definitely in shape and a great-looking guy back then. And it was true that months later she no longer thought of him as a creep. She said she found him different. How then was he able to change to a point where she could actually stand him?

Blake's mind, as tired as it was, even considered the possibility of Roy, if he was indeed Luann's 'R', ultimately becoming the psychopath who murdered Marcie and the other red-headed women. And Luann was a red-head herself. Could it be that Mr. R did run Luann off the road and his guilt with that turned him into a killer of red-headed women? Was the rag doll some kind of symbolic connection to the doll that he had won for Luann? Or the baby, *his* baby, that she gave up? If the man were Roy, Blake already knew the toy-master could get his hands on all the Raggedy Ann dolls he wanted. Blake's brain was on fire. Allowing his head to fall against the wingback, the words screamed in his head, "Why did you do this, Luann? Why did you betray our marriage? Why did you do this to Starr and me?"

There was a soft rapping on his bedroom door. "Dad, are you awake?"

Blake opened his eyes and glanced quickly at the clock radio. It was eight ten. The sun was peeking in from between the Venetian blind slats. He was still in the same position in the chair. The diary and pad had fallen to the floor.

"Come on in, Starr."

The door opened and a bewildered Starr appeared in shorts and a red UGA tee shirt. "I thought you were already up and gone; then I saw your door shut…"

"Just over-slept, that's all."

"You've been in the chair all night?"

"Guess so."

She noticed the diary on the floor. "I take it you went ahead and read it?"

Blake nodded. "It wasn't the most enjoyable novel I've ever read."

"Are you going in to work today?"

"I hadn't planned to. Bobby's on this morning. Linc is supposed to be down in Brunswick at a family reunion. I'm going in from four till eleven. So, I want you to stay the evening with Katie and Tommy."

"No, Dad. I don't want to go anywhere today."

"We *are* having Sunday dinner at Katie's after church. You need to be getting ready for Sunday School."

"I didn't plan to go today, Dad."

"Because of the scuttlebutt?"

"We walk into that church and everybody will be looking at us."

"That won't bother me. I'm surprised it will bother you."

"I'm not going to church, Dad. I'll go to Katie's with you for dinner, but I'm coming home afterwards."

"Starr, don't let the business of this diary get to you. I don't really care what the people about town are saying. We need to go on about our lives and put the thing behind us."

"It doesn't matter to you what everyone thinks about Mom?"

"Yeah. But what can either of us do about it?"

Starr didn't reply, but shook her head and walked away.

There wasn't much more to say at Katie's. Blake didn't want to bring up the topic again and Katie sensed it. Dinner was good. The atmosphere was sullen. The diary of a woman who had been dead ten years had put a family and a town to wonder. Who was the man of mystery and was he a killer living among them?

Blake took Starr home after dinner at her insistence. Before he left to relieve Bobby, he asked Mrs. Baker to keep a watchful eye out for her while he pulled duty.

Bobby was at his desk when Blake arrived just after four. "Boss, if you don't feel like working this evening, I don't mind pulling a double. It's not like I have anyone to go home to."

"No, you go on. By the way, Anna Mae tells me you're seeing some young thing over in Scottsdale."

"Well, she's not *that* young. She's twenty four. And yes, we're pretty tight. The only thing is: she hates going out on a date in the patrol car."

"Then get yourself a ride, man."

"Thinkin' about it. I just don't have a lot of capital right now."

"Go see Bessie Cotter's boy. He's got a good looking inventory and I hear he works with you on deals."

"Maybe I'll do that. You sure I can't stay on for you?"

"Nope. Go."

"Well, I *would* like to spend some time in Scottsdale tonight."

"Like I said. Go!"

Bobby stopped and turned before leaving out. "How are things at home? You know, with Starr and the diary thing."

"Fine, Bobby. We sorted it out."

"Well, get ready for the stares and questions out there."

Blake nodded. "Yeah."

At a quarter till five, Blake locked up and went on patrol. Turning onto Barnwell Street, he spotted Roy McIntyre's black Dodge Ram Powerwagon sitting in front of his business. Again the idea of Roy coming back into Luann's life entered his head. More importantly, if Roy was the man, did he have a hand in her death? Did the man bump her vehicle as he had done before and knock her off the bridge? For some reason, both the images of the red-headed Luann and Marcie Rose entered Blake's mind.

He pulled the Blazer in behind the Powerwagon. Could Bessie Cotter have been mistaken about the make of the black vehicle she saw? In the dark a Dodge may look like a Suburban to a near-sighted old woman looking through what was probably seventy-five year old distorted glass. Blake sat behind the vehicle for a while, left elbow on the door trim and fingers on his chin. Maybe he was speculating too much.

Roy's Toys was closed on Sunday, but Roy generally spent a couple of hours every Sunday catching up on his bookkeeping in the back. After contemplating how he would approach Roy, Blake got out of his truck and made his way to the front door of the store. It was locked as he expected, so he walked down the alley to the delivery door in the rear. Finding it locked as well, Blake banged loudly on the door. Within thirty seconds Roy's voice bellowed from inside. "Who is it?"

"It's Blake Ravenel, Roy. Can you open up?"

Blake heard the click of the deadbolt. The door opened slowly and Roy's balding head appeared. After he was satisfied it was Blake, he opened it wider. A .357 hung from his right hand.

"What the devil are you doing back here, Chief?"

"Relax, Roy." He saw the revolver. "You don't need that. Go put it away."

"Okay, but what do you want?"

"Can I come in?"

Roy jerked his head toward his office. That's the best he could do for an invitation.

"So, what brings you back here, Chief?" Roy asked, moving to the back of his desk.

"I just wanted to talk to you some more. And by the way, why is it always 'Chief?' Can't you call me Blake? For God's sake, Roy, we were classmates and even friends at one time."

"I guess 'were' is the operative word here, don't you think?"

"I know we had a blow up over Luann, but that was a long time ago. She's long since gone and you and I haven't had a civil word for one another for over twelve years."

"And that's my fault?"

"No, Roy. I just wanted us to clear the air. If we need to get things out in the open, then fine."

"Is that why you're here, to rehash old issues?"

Blake crossed his arms below his chest. "Not exactly."

Roy sat down in the leather desk chair. "Then what, Blake? What more *can* we say to one another. You're right. Luann's gone and we're both sorry about that. Nothing more either of us can say."

Blake looked down and shuffled his feet. Opening up this dialogue was not going to be easy.

Suddenly Roy sat up straight in his chair and grinned. "Damn. It just hit me. Debbie Young told me this morning about Starr's finding a diary Luann wrote. Some guy was getting Luann's best while you were in Vietnam, I hear. Some guy with the initial R. You think it's me, don't you?" He laughed loudly and slapped his hand down on the desk.

Blake didn't appreciate the laughter, but kept his tongue. "I don't know, Roy. I want to hear you say it wasn't you."

Roy laughed again, hysterically, but then just as quickly, dropped the corners of his mouth into a scowl. "That was funny for a minute, but I should be angry if anything. The talk is that Starr thinks Luann's lover may in fact have killed her and all those red-headed women as well. That could make me the killer, you think."

"I'm not accusing you of anything, Roy. I just want you to tell me it was not you who was with Luann in 1972. I said nothing about you being a murderer."

Roy stood and with dead-honest eyes said, "No, Blake. And this is for the record. I had nothing more to do with Luann after you went into service. Hell, I hardly saw her around town the whole time you were gone and when I did, we never spoke. And that's the God's truth."

Blake nodded. "Okay, Roy. Let's say I believe you. But I always wondered, though. Why is it you have never, to my knowledge, gone out with anyone?"

"Who says I haven't? And what's that got to do with anything?"

"I don't know. Maybe nothing. But if Luann was the last woman you went out with and then she dumped you...."

"Hmmm. And naturally I never got over it, so it ate away at me so long I waited for you to go to Vietnam and then I killed her. I became some goddam psychopath and killed all the other women because they had red hair like her. And because I own a toy store, I had access to all those Raggedy Ann dolls and planted them on the dead women. Gee, it all makes perfect sense to me. How about you?"

Blake didn't have the words to respond. Actually Roy did sum it all up very nicely, except for one thing. Blake actually did realize Roy wasn't Luann's lover nor was he the killer of the young women. Roy's facetious confession was nothing more than sarcasm and discordance. And Blake fully understood why Roy had an attitude. After all, he had barged in on the man and as much accused him.

But Roy also understood Blake's frustration and embarrassment from the diary gossip that was flooding the town. He hated it when women came into the store and spread their idle rumors and tales like pig manure.

"Look, Blake. I know you have a tough job and these murders are still hanging over your head. I hate it more'n you can imagine about Coach St. Clair's daughter. You asked me about the number of rag dolls sold in my store. I did go back through my receipts…back as far as 1979. I bet we didn't sell but three in the past three years. I believe they were all bought by mothers. See that box over there?" He pointed toward the corner of the room. "Full of Raggedy Ann dolls. I pulled them off the shelves the day after you all found that woman from Savannah behind Katie's. I hate sensationalism and curiosity seekers. Just felt it was in bad taste to leave them out."

Blake nodded. Today Roy was a different person from the man who in the last dozen years showed nothing but disdain for Blake. Either Roy was giving Blake the best snow job he'd ever gotten or he was actually a straight up guy who along with Blake allowed the differences of the past to perpetuate their discord over the years. Both men realized that their pride had stood in the way of ever reconciling and reconstituting their friendship.

Blake held out his hand and Roy took it. They still exchanged only looks, not words. But it was a start. Perhaps the next time they saw one another, the words would be there. Friendly words.

CHAPTER THIRTEEN

It was now after seven and Blake sat in his office mulling over his conversation with Roy. Okay, if he could believe Roy, that he was not Luann's R man, then who was? Blake was convinced it had to be someone from the Pine River area. But was the man still around? And there was no tangible proof that Luann's lover went off the deep end and later began killing women with red hair. He was back to square one with that. But what about the California and Vegas killings with the same M.O.? His head was spinning again. Try as he may, he just couldn't connect all the dots.

Blake picked up the phone and dialed out. "You doing okay, sweetheart?

"Yes, Daddy. When are you coming home?"

"I don't know. I may try to get out of here early. Got a lot of reports to catch up on, though. Just make sure the door is locked and don't open it for anyone except Mrs. Baker. She's supposed to check on you."

"I'll be fine, Daddy. I'm going to bed early anyway. Just so tired these last few days."

"I can't imagine why. 'Bye."

Returning to the cumbersome task of his semi-annual report to the town council, he rubbed his tired eyes. Blake had gotten his wrist slapped at the Saturday meeting for not having it in on the due date, July 15th. More and more the paper chase was bogging him down. The myriad of reports to the state, county and town each month stole away valuable time that could be otherwise utilized to provide service and protection to Pine River.

At nine-twenty the phone rang. On the line was the excited voice of an anonymous male calling from a phone booth adjacent to where he was witnessing a burglary at Hyman's on the west edge of town. Blake grabbed his keys, locked the station door behind him and scrambled to the Blazer. As Bobby was probably in Scottsdale and Linc, on his way back from Brunswick, Blake switched frequencies and called county for back-up.

"This is Ravenel in Pine River. We have a four-five-nine in progress at Hyman's Furniture on 4th Street. Can you assist?"

"Stand by," the voice responded.

"Roger. Two officers on the way and will meet you at the 20."

The only problem was, he would arrive at the store a full ten minutes before the deputies would get to the scene.

Blake rode Code 2 through the streets at a break-neck

clip, until he reached 4th at which time he killed the lights. Pulling his shotgun from the dash, he laid his flashlight atop the barrel and proceeded cautiously toward the store. The front door glass had been smashed and the door itself stood ajar. By the time County would arrive, the perp may be finished with business and gone. The time to move in was now.

At the door Blake could see that the alarm had been cut. Being careful not to step on the broken glass, which would make a crunching sound and announce his presence, he took a giant step that placed him inside the store. He heard no lights or noises. The store was deathly quiet except for the ticking of a grandfather clock somewhere off to the right. He aimed the beam of his light throughout every part of the large showroom, hoping to alarm the intruder, but it generated no activity. Either the burglar had hit and run or was in the office at the rear of the store where the safe was located. Blake moved forward toward the back room, checking behind couches and wardrobes on the way. The quiet was deafening, not to mention eerie.

******

At twenty minutes till ten Starr was in bed. Although her hot bath served to be therapeutic, she still felt like she was twelve going on fifty. Her brain was tired and her eyes were still burning from reading and re-reading the diary. She guessed her dad had put it away somewhere and with all of the hullabaloo around town about it, if she never saw it again, it would be too soon.

Through the palladium, light from the half moon illuminated the room with the same softness of a night light. The popping and cracking of the house as it was cooling down from the day's oppressive heat always seemed more pronounced at night, especially when her dad was not around. Not since she was a small child, however, had she been afraid to stay by herself. She always knew her dad was close by somewhere and the town itself was as safe as a mother's arms. And tonight the moonlight poured into the room like an old friend, warming, calming, soothing. High up on the dresser Annie sat with her back against the mirror, making it appear there were two of her. In the diluted light her frozen smile haunted the room.

Starr began to fade as her eyes blinked open to closed, open to closed, until she was nearly under. Another slight pop of the flooring opened her heavy lids just enough to see the gloved hand as it moved swiftly over her mouth. Her heart jumped into her throat and she tried to scream. But the hand was strong, covering all of her mouth and part of her nose. Straining her eyes upward, she could barely make out the hooded figure in black. Thoughts of imminent death swarmed through her mind. He was there to kill her. Starr tried to struggle from his grasp to no avail. Her screams were muffled beneath the glove and tears of bridling fear formed in her eyes, distorting further view of the intruder.

His guttural voice whispered in her ear. "Do you know who I am?"

Starr shook her head furiously trying to wrench free from his grip at the same time. She smelled the cologne on his glove.

"I will take my hand away if you tell me you won't scream. Nod if you agree."

Starr nodded once and he released his hand.

In the dimly lit room she could only see the man's silhouette. She tried to make out his eyes through the two small openings in the mask, but could not.

"The diary," the voice whispered. "Where is it?"

"I don't…I don't have it," she stammered.

"Don't lie to me!" The man's voice, now elevated sounded venomous, like Satan himself. "I'll ask you again, where is it?"

Starr gulped. "I'm telling you the truth. My dad took it."

"Okay." The voice was again whispering. "Then tell me, little girl, did that mother of yours mention me by name?"

Now she knew. Her mother's killer was not only still in Pine River, but was standing over her. Finding just the smallest iota of courage, she replied, "If I knew who you were, I would tell you."

The intruder grabbed Starr by the shoulders and sat her up in bed. "It's not my business to kill little girls, Starr Ravenel, but with you I can make an exception. Answer my question *now*!"

Her bravery was short-lived. She had no doubt he would indeed kill her if she toyed with him. "If it is *you* in the diary, she only referred to you as R."

The man threw her forcefully back to her pillow and pulled a gleaming knife from a sheath on his belt. Holding the tip close to her jugular, he said, "Now you listen good, kid. Don't think of trying to find me out. You let the past stay dead along with your mother. If you persist in playing detective, I will come back here and kill you where you sleep. And next time there will be no warning." The whisper became even more diabolical. "You do know what I'm capable of, don't you, Starr. Just ask Marcie. Oh, I'm sorry, Marcie's dead. "

Starr's eyes were wild with fear. She nodded her head rapidly several times.

The killer leaned down within a foot from her face. She closed her eyes tightly, then screamed as he grabbed her hair and sliced away one of her curls. As she lay with her hands over her face, sobbing, he stood and walked to the dresser. Annie's black eyes and painted smile seemed to mock him. Starr opened her eyes and saw him pick up the doll. "Your mother. I loved her, you know." He brought the doll up to his face and kissed it through the mask. "She died quickly. I didn't intend for it to happen. But she ran away. Nobody runs from *me*, Starr. *Nobody*!"

As quickly as he had appeared, he was gone.

Chills worked up and down her spine in glissando fashion. Trying to digest the nightmare, she sat for several moments shaking. The tears began again, only now these were tears of relief.

******

There was no one in the store. The door to the office was locked and did not appear to have been jimmied. There was no way of telling if anything had been stolen. Only Mr. Hyman would know after a walk-through and an inventory. Blake found the master switch and turned on the lights. To Blake everything looked in place. In fact, nothing was disturbed and there was no evidence save the broken door glass that the place had been burglarized.

He walked to the front door just as the county deputies were arriving. The blue flashing light on their patrol car created a strobe effect in the adjacent store front windows. Blake signaled to them with his flashlight and they entered the store.

"If there actually was a B&E here, it doesn't appear there was any *entering*," he told the officers. "Could have just been vandalism, but someone supposedly called from that booth across the street and said he was actually witnessing a break-in. I wonder…."

Blake went to a phone at a sales desk and dialed his house. A whimper of a voice answered.

"Starr. I'm sorry, honey. Did I wake you up?"

"Daddy!!" she screamed. "Come home now! A man…. he broke in and….he grabbed me, Daddy. He said he was going to kill me."

"Starr, is this for real? This is not one of your shenanigans…."

When all she did was sob on the phone instead of answering him, Blake yelled back into the receiver, "Is he still in the house?"

Again, just sobbing.

"Don't worry; I'll be there as quick as I can. Don't cry, sweetheart. I'm coming now."

Blake was frantic. "Fellows, I have an emergency at home. Can you get hold of the owner? His name is Hyman, like on the sign. Ben Hyman on Carolina Street I think. See if he can come down here and secure the place. Tell him I'll come back later. Thanks." He ran out the door, jumped into the Blazer and peeled out in the direction of his house at break-neck speed. As he straightened out the corners, he prayed to God Starr was all right. Was this for real? He knew she was laced with high-jinx, but she would never pull such a 'cry wolf' stunt.

Within three long minutes he was home. Springing from the truck, he didn't even take time to shut his door. When he leapt over the pair of steps up to the porch, he froze in horror. Starr's doll, Annie, was impaled through the neck by an ice pick that was nailed to the door. Blake left the doll where it was and turned the front door knob. It was unlocked. Apparently, Starr had not come back downstairs to re-lock it. With gun in hand, he bounded the stairs three at a time and advanced to her room. Through the open door he positioned himself in a crouch and swept his Glock around the room until it stopped in line with Starr's headboard.

She was not in her bed or anywhere else in the room. Maybe she ran out of the house. But then he thought. "She wouldn't do that."

"Starr. Where are you?" he called.

There was no answer at first. Then he heard what sounded like a muffled cry from the closet. Upon pushing open the bi-fold, he found her sitting against the wall, knees up under her chin and arms cradling her legs. "Daddy," she whispered. He holstered the gun and gathered her up in his arms.

"Are you all right, sweetheart?" he asked, softly.

Starr nodded. "It was horrible, Daddy. I just knew he was going to kill me."

Blake placed her on the bed and sat down beside her. "Did you get a good look at him?"

Starr shook her head. "It was kind of dark and he was wearing a black mask. He was all in black." She began to regain her composure and dried her eyes with a corner of her sheet.

"How about his voice? Could you make it out?"

"No. He whispered. He sounded like the devil in the Exorcist."

"Is there anything…anything at all that you remember he said or did that was significant?"

"No. Except…"

"Except what?"

"His cologne. I remember what it smelled like. I can't remember though if I smelled it in a store or on somebody. But I'll never forget it."

Blake caressed her leg and looked away. "I'm sorry I was not here for you, Starr. I think I was set up by this guy. How stupid can I be?"

"What do you mean?" she asked.

"I think the man who was here tonight smashed the door at Hyman's and called me to say it was being burglarized. It was an effective ruse. The guy's smart, I'll give him that." He paused. "You said on the phone that he threatened to kill you. What did he say exactly?"

Starr conveyed the entire conversation while Blake sat with mouth agape.

"So he says he was your mom's...friend."

"Yes. And he was here looking for the diary. I think he was afraid Mom wrote enough about him that someone could figure out who he is. Then he admitted he rammed Mom's car. That's why she went off the bridge. He murdered her, Dad. And another thing...he as much bragged he killed Marcie and the other women."

Blake put both hands to his forehead and covered his face. "Holy shit. And he could just as easily hurt you. Or worse."

"He said he's not in the business of killing children, but said he would make an exception if I found out who he was."

Blake's eyes turned angry and fierce. "You won't be finding out, but by God, *I* will."

They were silent for a few moments, then Starr said, "Dad, he took my Annie."

"Don't worry, Starbright. I found it outside." He

would not tell her *how* he found it. He knew it was placed there as a warning. Somehow the killer knew that Starr was smart *and* extremely tenacious. If anyone could figure out who he was, it would be her. The warning was for her not to probe any further. Blake surmised it was a warning for *him* as well. Now it was for certain: neither Rupert Kolb nor Jake Thigpen was the killer. Kolb was just an unfortunate soul and Thigpen was just caught in an unfortunate situation.

The next morning when Blake backed from his driveway, he saw Mary Alice Baker in her housecoat retrieving the Gazette from her front lawn. In less than five minutes the timer would set off the sprinkler system and soak the paper. Blake stopped at the edge of the street, rolled down his window and called to her.

"Morning, Blake," she replied, pulling together the upper part of her garment as though she were actually showing something. "Excuse my looks."

"Mrs. Baker, you were watching out for Starr last night."

"Yes, and glad to do it."

"You checked on her about eight-thirty, I understand."

She nodded. "That's about right. Is there a problem?"

"Someone broke in just before ten and attacked Starr."

She gasped, dropped the Gazette, and placed her hand over her breasts. "What?! Attacked? What do you mean attacked?"

"A man in a mask wanted that diary everyone's talking about. He thought Starr knew who he was from what Luann wrote. Mrs. Baker, he threatened to kill her."

"Oh my God, Blake. I can't believe it. She was fine when I went by and I made sure the door was locked when I left. What in the world is happening in this town? Two murders and a little girl attacked! Has Satan taken up residence in Pine River?"

"Did you look across the street between say nine-thirty and ten last night?"

"I did. Several times." She sounded a little defensive.

"And you didn't see anybody or anything suspicious?"

"No. Nothing." Now very defensive.

Realizing there was a bit of ire in his voice, he apologized. "Sorry, Mrs. Baker. I didn't mean to sound ungrateful. I know you've been looking out for her every day and you do it so freely. I've just been upset about what happened to her."

"And rightly so. From now on, you bring her here to stay during the day. She'll be good company for me now that Mr. Baker passed last year."

"Oh, I couldn't impose on you like that. I'll just detail Linc and Bobby to cruise by more often. And she'll stay at Mrs. Bledsoe's in the evenings when I'm on duty." He smiled and nodded. "Have a pleasant day, Mrs. Baker. Thanks."

Blake called the County D.A. and filled him in on the incident at the house. "I think you can release Jake now. Obviously, he didn't kill Marcie and definitely not the other women."

"I don't know, Chief. I hate what happened to your little girl, but I can't let the boy go based on her claim that he said he murdered the St. Clair girl. The fact is, Thigpen was *with* the girl, his semen was in her and as far as the county is concerned, he was the *last* person with her. I think we'll hang on to him. We'll just see what kind of case we got come the hearing. You catch the man you think did the killing and get a confession. Then Thigpen will walk."

Later that morning, when he was in the station alone, Blake retrieved Luann's diary from his briefcase and photocopied most of it. It took the better part of an hour. He then took out an Express Mail envelope and addressed it to Special Agent Puckett in the Savannah FBI office. Inside was a note:

> *Agent Puckett,*
> *You will find the contents of this journal interesting. We will have already talked about the diary and the attack on my daughter by the time you get this. I am confident the 'rag doll' killer we are looking for is the man you will read about. Call me after you read this.*
> *Regards,*
> *Blake Ravenel*
> *Pine River*

After plastering the envelope with five stamps and writing "Confidential. To be opened by addressee only", he dropped it in the mailbox outside of his office. Returning straight-away to his desk, he called Puckett and filled him in on the events of the past days. Actually hearing himself discussing Luann's infidelity and her probable murder was immensely upsetting to him.

"Thanks, Blake. I know this was difficult for you, but it's the first real break we've had on the case. If this guy in the diary is truly our killer, we may be able to extract enough information to develop a profile."

The days were quiet and uneventful the last two weeks of August. On the twenty-seventh the kids went back to school. Starr suddenly became popular with students who the school year before never gave her the time of day. Even Suze Effingham, the pixie-cute blonde Head Cheerleader and her co-blonde entourage wanted to be Starr's friends. After all, Starr was famous, being the talk of the town in finding the mystery diary and then attacked in her own bed and living to tell about it. Tommy Lee sat at a table all to himself at lunch looking rather dejected. But as fickle as girls can be, two days later Starr was no longer an icon with the blondie bunch and she was back at Tommy Lee's table.

Sanger Stadium had never held the number of fans as it did in the season opener the first Friday night in September, 1982. The remarkable thing was, the Rebels were going to be fortunate to win a game. All but two of the starters on the 1981 seven-and-four squad had graduated. But the people of Pine River had turned out to support the Saint, their coach. He was the only coach most could remember. Even the old timers had forgotten the great years of the Roland Sanger dynasty in the Forties. And even if this team got killed every week, there would be no talk about how 'sorry' the squad was. Nor would there be a discussion that perhaps it was time Charlie St. Clair retired. Many of the town folk had not seen Coach all summer. Some would be there for curiosity or to pity him, but all were there *for* him. For them and their beleaguered town a first game win would be a shot in the arm. A town that had endured the most powerful tornado ever in South Georgia, and of course the tragic loss of one of its most precious children.

Blake stood beside his mentor on the sidelines watching the Long County team dismantle the Rebels. His heart ached for Charlie St. Clair. He wished he could somehow turn back the clock to 1968, suit up, and with his pin-point passing, take his Rebels downfield for at least one score. At half-time Pine River was down 33-0. The night would get longer.

When it was over and the Saint left the field with his team, head down and shoulders slumped, most of the fans that had stuck it out in respect for the man, gave him a standing ovation. There were no boos for the dejected team even though they had taken it on the chin to the tune of 59-7. Win or lose, they would all be back.

Blake leaned against the wall in the tunnel outside the dressing room listening for Coach to rip the losers apart. He remembered how St. Clair would spit out his combination of obscenities and humiliations that made the boys feel lower than a snake's belly, even if they trounced the opposing team. Blake waited to hear the words through the locker room door, something like: "So how is it the other team showed up to play football while you sorry-asses played goddam tiddly-winks? And you girls on the offensive line. I counted sixteen missed blocks tonight. You couldn't hit water if you fell out of a goddam boat!"

Standing with arms crossed and smiling, time tumbled back for Blake. He missed it all, badly. He missed the Coach's berating as well as his wit and humor. Coach was more 'Patton' than Patton was. Blake waited for the voice. The powerful voice was soon to echo through the dressing room, into the corridor and heard two streets over.

But tonight the great general of yesterday's Rebel army was not in that locker room. An older, sad, soft-spoken man, however, was. Straining his ears, what Blake heard instead was: "You fellas did your best out there tonight. They were just better'n us, that's all. We'll get 'em next week. See you Monday at practice. Go get some sleep now, boys."

Blake thought he was going to cry. The man's spirit was gone. Someone had robbed the coach of his very soul when Marcie was taken from him. Blake turned and walked from the door down the dark corridor. He banged his fist on the concrete wall just before entering the parking lot. Starr, Katie and Tommy Lee had long since left the stadium and would be waiting for him at the Bledsoe house.

On Sunday after church, Katie and Tommy Lee came to Blake's for dinner. When they arrived, Starr and Blake were in the kitchen frying chicken. As Blake was no cook and Starr was just learning, most of their meals were popped in the microwave.

"Do we need to call the fire department?" Katie asked, fanning the smoke from her face. "Here. Let me help. You know I *am* a professional. First thing, turn down the burner and turn on the fan. By the way, chief, you look cute in that apron." She gave him a quick peck on the lips.

At that moment there was a knock at the front door. Starr broke loose from the kitchen to see who it was. "Do you think it's Ed McMahon?" she jested. Upon opening the door to merely a crack, the last person she ever thought would be standing on their front porch, rendered her speechless.

"Hello, Miss. Is your father home?"

"Uh…hello Mr. Kolb," she responded, not allowing the door to open further than a couple of feet. "Please wait here and I'll get him."

She walked back to the kitchen and mouthed in an animated whisper, "It's Rupert Kolb from next door."

Blake raised his eyebrows and quickly cast the apron aside. "Interesting," he said, moving to the front door.

"Mr. Kolb. What can I do for you?"

The man stood with his hands in his pocket and in an almost apologetic tone he said, "I don't want to impose, sir, but is there a place we can talk?"

"Yes. Yes, come in."

Kolb stepped in and smelling the chicken, said "I'm sorry, you're having dinner."

"That's all right. We're not ready to eat yet. The bird may not even be edible. Pardon the smoke." He gestured to his left. "Let's go to the parlor. Can I offer you some coffee or a soft drink?"

"No, thank you."

Kolb sat in the sofa chair and looked around the room. "Very nice place, Mr. Ravenel."

Blake nodded. "Thanks." He waited for Kolb to come to the point of his visit.

"I came to turn myself in. It's time now."

Blake frowned. "Turn yourself in? For what?"

"I suppose 'accessory after the fact, aiding and abetting.' Probably a lot of other crimes as well, like 'obstruction of justice.'"

"I don't understand, Mr. Kolb. What are you referring to?" Blake stood and closed the French doors to the hallway.

"My name is Burt Morris, Chief. Several years ago my twin brother, Stanley, murdered his wife and two daughters. I don't know why and for that matter, he probably didn't either. You see, he disappeared after the murders for maybe three years; then one day he ended up on my doorstep. He was a broken man. I hardly recognized him and found he definitely wasn't in his right mind. He asked me to help him. I knew he was sick in the mind and something had to be done for him. I didn't want him to go to jail, although he would probably have been institutionalized. I have no doubt he would have been found insane." Kolb paused and took out a handkerchief to wipe his eyes. "I decided to hide him out for a while, but ended up having him committed under the name Stanley Kolb, like the name I took. It was psychiatric care he needed, Chief. Not jail."

Blake listened intently, shaking his head. "How did you manage to pay for the care?"

"I lived for a while with the woman you asked me about, Bonnie Wagner. She had some money and really couldn't much take care of herself. I was disabled and lived on a pension, but I didn't tell her about it. She also paid me for the work I did around her place. I chauffeured her around, did her grocery shopping and anything else she needed. I'm ashamed to admit it, but I also did sexual favors, too."

Blake didn't comment. He kept his unwavering eyes fixed on the man.

"You see I'm a Korean War vet. Got shot up pretty bad at Chosin. I didn't tell Bonnie about my pension, because I had it paid to me in an allotment that went directly to the psychiatric hospital to keep my brother. It took every bit of it."

Kolb stopped his soliloquy for a few moments and looked away toward the window. The wind had picked up and distant thunder announced an approaching storm.

He finally continued. "About the time Bonnie died, I found that a police detective had been following up on a tip from people who said they saw Stanley in a hardware store in Tinton Falls. Well, actually, that was me they saw. I figured it was time to move on. Bonnie left me her savings which was over a hundred thousand. I pulled Stanley out of the hospital and moved him to Savannah. Put him in the Charter System there. By the time we came down here, he didn't even know who I was. Most of the time he would just sit in a chair and look out the window without moving an eyelash. I moved to Pine River so I could be close and go check on him once or twice a week."

Blake sat pulling at his bottom lip, hanging on every word. "Mr. Kolb…I guess I should now call you Morris…. I don't know what to say. I do think you may have realized when I called you in that I was fishing for information about you and these very New Jersey killings. It wasn't just about Marcie St. Clair's murder. But you were pretty evasive, even defensive."

"Why on earth would you think I killed that girl anyway?"

"It wasn't that I really suspected you, but you do own a vehicle that resembles the SUV a witness saw on the road where Marcie was last seen. But actually it was my daughter Starr, who by the way thinks she's a junior G-man, who found a picture of your brother in newspaper archives. She aged the photo by sketching what he'd look like twenty years later and thought for sure it was you. I can't believe she was almost right."

"She's a smart kid, all right. I actually thought she might be onto me. I knew she and that boy were watching me. I admit I did my best to make them a bit uneasy by staring back at them. Of course, I never meant any harm by it. I would never mean any harm to *anybody*."

"So, Mr. Morris. Why did you decide to finally turn yourself in?"

"It was just time, Mr. Ravenel. I had done all I could to protect my brother. I knew his mind wasn't right; otherwise, he would never have killed his precious family." He dabbed his eyes again. "I buried him yesterday. An orderly at the hospital said Stanley was sitting on the front porch Thursday, got up on his own and walked down to the reflection pool. He stepped into the water and drowned himself. He had sat in one position for more than ten years with that same terrified expression on his face. No one ever expected him to move a muscle, much less get out of his chair. No one thought to watch him.

"My obligation to my brother has ended, Chief. I'm now ready to accept what's coming to me."

The man's story had been compelling and Blake could see that he was a sad and troubled man. But he could also see something in his face he had not seen before. Relief. He had indeed broken the law, but out of love and a sense of obligation for his brother. Blake really didn't know what to do with him.

"I'll not arrest you today, Mr. Morris. I want you to have the day to grieve for your brother. You go home and stay there until you hear from me. Tomorrow I will make a call to the Trenton PD to tell them they can finally close the long chapter on their homicide. It will be up to them as to what will be done with you."

Morris stood and offered his hand to Blake. He took it, then placed his other hand on the man's shoulder to escort him to the door. "Go on home, Mr. Morris. I know you probably have some affairs to get in order." Blake watched with heavy heart as Morris dragged his game leg down the sidewalk toward his house in the now pouring rain. Like the smash of a cymbal followed by the dramatic roll of kettle drums, a clap of thunder seemed to add that long awaited crescendo to Burt Morris' tragic opera.

As soon as he left, Starr bounded from the kitchen with, as expected, a curious face. "What did he want, Dad?"

"Peace, my dear." He didn't elaborate further, but strode past his confused daughter to the kitchen and the burnt chicken. "Anybody up for the Western Sizzler?"

That night Blake found Starr sitting as usual in her spot on the window seat, gown wrapped tightly around her feet, windows flung wide open. The afternoon's thunderstorm had cleansed the air and the night sky was dotted with luminous stars. He perched himself beside her and peered through the telescope at Mars.

"Do you think my Mom's in Heaven, Daddy?"

He pulled away from the eyepiece and studied her sparkling eyes in the dim light. "I suppose so, Starr. She's probably talking with God right now."

"Do you think Marcie's there with her?"

"I don't have all the answers. These are things only God knows. But I can only guess she'd be up there too."

"Reverend Kelly said everyone who gets to Heaven will have a new, perfect body. I didn't see anything wrong with their old bodies. Do you think God will let them keep their red hair?"

Blake smiled. Starr was a virtual enigma. Sometimes she conversed with the intellectual maturity of a science professor, while at other times she was like a six year old with the questions. "You know what I think? I think that smart little brain of yours wonders too much about things and its time to shut it down for the night."

He swept her up in his arms and deposited her in bed. She fluffed up her pillow and crawled beneath the covers.

"Goodnight, Starbright."

"Goodnight, Daddy."

He turned to leave the room.

"Daddy?"

"Yes?"

"Would you tuck me in?"

Blake returned to her bedside and brought the covers up under her chin. "Are you too big for your old dad to kiss you goodnight?"

"No," she giggled.

The next morning at nine, Blake called Captain Bannister in Trenton. He could actually sense the release in the captain's voice. And truly, it was as though an albatross had been lifted from Bannister's neck. He said he could finally get a good night's sleep, and furthermore would be talking to his wife about retiring soon. Lastly, he had no interest in charging Burt Morris for accessory or obstruction. Through the years, the man had probably punished himself a thousand times over.

CHAPTER FOURTEEN

On the ninth of September, just after Blake arrived at the station, Anna Mae buzzed him. "Agent Lanham on the line, Blake."

"Yes, John?"

"Chief, can you meet over here at five this evening. Got a big task force pow-wow on these rag doll murders. Puckett will be here as will Savannah P.D. and your Sheriff Harper. I think we've finally got a profile on the killer. In talking with Harper today, I also think your county D.A. is going to drop the charges on the Thigpen boy."

"Good. It's about time. As for the meeting, I believe I can make it, but first I have to make arrangements for someone to look after my daughter this evening. I have a feeling we won't be done in an hour or two."

"Yeah, we've blocked off about three hours for the meeting. By the way, I heard it was probably the actual killer who broke into your house and threatened your girl. Is that right?"

"Looks that way, John. He said he was the one who killed Marcie St. Clair. I guess we will have to buy it for now. And...he admitted ramming my wife's car and knocking her off the bridge in '73."

"Oh, hell. The bastard killed your wife, too? We'll have to see how that configures in the profile. That means he was somewhere around your town at least ten years ago. I *know* you want to get this guy, now. Probably worse than anyone.

"More than you realize."

Blake called the diner for Katie and a very curt Minnie said she was home sick with the flu. And a bus load of senior citizens from Washington Village was coming in for lunch. How she was going to manage the crowd was beyond her. What a day for Katie to be sick. Blake thanked her and got off the phone as quickly as he could. He was in no mood to hear the woman bitch.

"Hello," Katie answered in her infected voice.

"It's Blake. Heard you were sick."

"I'd have to die to feel better."

"Sorry. Anything I can bring you? Hot chicken soup, maybe?"

"No, thanks. I'm taking some Tussin and drinking orange juice. I'll be okay in a couple of months. Did you want something?"

"Naw, I was just seeing if you could let Starr stay there

for the evening. I have to go to Savannah for a meeting. But now that I know you have the flu, I'll get Mrs. Baker to keep her."

"Probably best all around. She doesn't need my germs."

"Neither do I. Guess I'll keep away too."

Katie coughed a few times. "Are you sure you don't want to come over and do some kissy face? Then you can be just as miserable as me."

"I'll pass this time. But will take a rain check."

"I see. You're one of those rainy day guys."

"Hope you feel better. I'll check on you tonight when I get back."

Blake went out to the squad room to where Anna Mae and Bobby were. "I have to go to Savannah for a meeting this afternoon and likely won't be back until nine or ten. Starr was going to come by here anyway after school to stay till I was off duty. Will you two watch her for a while? And Bobby, when you get off shift, take her by Mrs. Baker's. I'll have her watch Starr till I get home."

"I'd be glad to look after her myself," Bobby offered, "but I'm going over to Scottsdale for supper at six."

"That's okay, Mrs. Baker will be glad to keep her tonight." He immediately got her on the phone.

"Oh, wonderful," she said. "We'll make fudge and just be a couple of girls."

Just before Blake left at four, Starr came into the station. He explained she would have to stay with Mrs.

Baker, but he would be home as quickly as he could. "Now you and I have beepers. Make sure you only call me if anything is wrong."

"Yes, yes, I know." She had already settled in at Linc's desk and taken her sketchpad out of her book bag.

"And Bobby, before you leave, check in with Linc. He's coming on at seven.

"Yes, yes. I know," he said, mimicking Starr.

Blake pointed playfully at him on the way out. "There's already one smart-ass in here; we don't need another."

After a half hour or so of working over her sketchpad with a charcoal pencil, Starr stood up to get more of a wide-angled perspective of her product.

"What are you drawing, kiddo?" Bobby leaned over her and saw the likeness of Anna Mae. "Ah. You've got her pegged all right. Right down to those cat eye glasses." He pinched Starr's cheek.

Starr slowly laid down her pencil and sat for a moment very still as though she were in deep thought. Bobby went back to his desk and then noticed that her face was pale and expressionless. Nearly catatonic. "You don't look so hot, Starbright? Are you sick? You didn't catch Katie's bug, did you?"

She looked quickly at both Anna Mae and Bobby, then walked briskly and without word out of the station house.

Anna Mae cast a bewildered look at Bobby. "So what got into her? She looked like she just saw a ghost. That poor girl just hasn't been actin' right since that monster got to her."

Bobby shrugged. "I guess I'd better go after her and get her to Mrs. Baker's. Blake will be mighty upset if we let her out of our sight."

But Starr already *was* out of sight.

The task force commenced its meeting promptly at five. Special Agent Puckett kicked-off the conference with a slide show. Graphic photographs of not only the four South Georgia victims, but the California and Vegas murder photos were incorporated as well. It appeared obvious that the throats were cut with the serrated edge of the same or similar blade, identical Raggedy Ann dolls placed beside or upon the bodies, and each victim having had recent sexual intercourse.

"We believe the killer is actually from Pine River, and thanks to Blake here for some new information that turned up a couple of weeks ago, we think the first woman he killed was either by accident or design."

Blake displayed some uneasiness and dropped his eyes to the papers on his lap.

Puckett continued. "He had an affair with a married woman, she became pregnant and then to his vehement objection, she had an abortion. She also broke it off with him. This apparently enraged him to a point where not only threatened her, but caused her death. We're dealing with a complex personality here. He's a man who has both a controlling Narcisstic and Antisocial nature, refuses to accept rejection, and is clinically psychopathological. We think that after the woman's death, he packed up and moved west. The women he killed apparently resembled the Pine River woman right down to the red hair. I believe the Raggedy Ann dolls left on the victims, which by the way is the same type of doll he bought for the woman's little girl, represents the aborted fetus, his own child. Killing these women somehow momentarily takes away the pain of his loss and redeems him for the sin of killing his first real love."

Blake was now hiding his emotions with a hand over his face. He hadn't looked at the agent the entire time he was speaking.

Lanham looked at the others and shook his head. "Is all this supported by Bureau psychologists or your own analysis?"

"A little of both, Agent Lanham," replied Puckett. "I agree it sounds a bit bizarre, but it's classic. The man's a true psychopath."

Blake finally looked up. "Jim, what will this guy look like?"

"Well, it's hard to say, but we know at least ten years ago he was strong and athletic, very nice looking, charismatic to a fault, now in his early thirties, knows how to handle a knife, could be a surgeon or even a butcher. With his looks and charm, he's easily able to gain the confidence and lull a vulnerable woman into a compromising situation. Most of all, he's a predator, as they all are."

Suddenly, a bad feeling came over Blake as he listened

to Agent Puckett's synopsis. He was worried about Starr and hated he had to be away from her. He checked his beeper, but apparently she had not needed to contact him. It was now after six and would be dark in a couple of hours. The meeting would probably go on for at least another hour. He thought once or twice about calling her, but she was supposed to be at Mrs. Baker's by now. He would call the woman's house when the meeting broke up.

Starr had not gone to Mrs. Baker's house as her dad told her. Instead, she went to Katie's. No one was at home. Katie was supposed to be sick at home. Where was she? Katie's friend and next door neighbor, Janet Englehoff, saw Starr on the front porch and yelled to her. "Katie's not home, dear! She was pretty sick today and left a few minutes ago for the 24 hour clinic! She ought to be back in an hour or so!"

Instead of going to Mrs. Baker's as her dad had instructed, Starr decided to sit and wait for Katie in the back yard swing. She really needed to talk to her. Holding the beeper in her hand, she could see her dad had not called her. She couldn't call him as he would be in the middle of his conference. Katie would be home soon.

It was now eight o'clock and Katie was not back. Starr knew she couldn't wait any longer. It was nearly dark. Running as fast as she could, she crossed Park to Main and then to Jefferson where she ended up on the Baker porch. After ringing her doorbell a half dozen times, she found that Mary Alice Baker was not home either. Starr knew that her dad had arranged with Mrs. Baker for her to stay there until he came home. Maybe she had an emergency. But she would have left a note.

Starr finally crossed the street and put in her key to unlock the door. But it was not locked. She knew her dad locked it when they left for him to take her to school. She flipped the wall switch to turn on the hall light, but it was out. Fear began to grip her, much as it did when she was accosted in her bedroom. She moved to the parlor and reached along the wall to flip the switch by the French doors.

Suddenly the front door opened. She had neglected to lock it when she came in. Standing in the hallway was Rupert Kolb, or whatever his name was.

"Y...you!" she stammered. He moved toward her and she backed into the hall table. His face, vaguely discernible in the faint ray of the streetlight, was still frightening. The eyes were fierce and his expression, chilling.

"What are you doing in our house? Please. Don't hurt me." Her voice quaked in fear.

Burt Morris then put his index finger over his lips as if to warn her to be quiet. From the dark living room on the opposite side of the hall, a shadowy figure sprang onto Morris, spinning him around. As Morris lunged at him, Starr heard a sickening thud. Morris reeled and fell hard onto the wood floor. Starr ran into the parlor and groped her way to the table lamp by the couch. When the knob clicked, the room illuminated.

She could see Morris lying face down on the floor, blood oozing from his forehead. From the hall shadows appeared the intruder, dressed as he had been before, all in black and wearing a black hood. In his hand was the gun that he had apparently used to bludgeon Morris.

Starr took a deep breath and found the words to challenge the man. "You don't need the mask any longer, Bobby. I know who you are."

Startled at Starr's revelation, Bobby pulled off the hood. "How did you know, Starbright?"

"Don't call me that again. I only let my close friends call me Starbright, not psycho murderers like you."

"Tsk, tsk, little one. No need to get nasty about this."

"So why did you kill all those women?"

Bobby walked toward her, slowly. "You know what has to happen now. Why couldn't you just be a little girl and not play detective?"

Starr didn't answer. She had been taking short backward steps toward the kitchen where she would be in position to bolt out the back door.

"Eh, eh," he warned, pointing his Beretta in her direction. "Stay right where you are."

She stopped at the fireplace.

"I'll ask you again. How did you know?"

"Your cologne, psycho. I smelled it on you when you put your hand over my mouth. That's the one real thing that stayed with me. I just couldn't remember where I smelled it before. Then when you bent over me this afternoon at the station, I smelled it again. I've never smelled it on anyone else."

Bobby laughed. It was almost a fiendish laugh. "I thought when I saw the way you were looking at me it was something like that. Foiled and betrayed by my *Homme*." He moved closer to Starr, the gun trained onto her head. "Your mother liked the cologne, Starr. Said it drove her crazy." He smiled and his eyes took on a glazed expression as though he were remembering their interludes.

Starr feigned that she was becoming comfortable with their conversation, partly because she didn't want him to kill her, but also because she had designs on the fireplace poker behind her. "My mom didn't mention your name in the diary, so your little visit to my bedroom was unnecessary. If you hadn't done that, you may have never been found out. She did refer to you as R. So tell me, Bobby, why R?"

"She liked calling me Robert. That's what my mother called me." His eyes trailed off to the right, giving the impression he was revisiting his childhood. His lips were quivering. "I did love your mother, Starr. And I know she loved me, too."

"Don't talk about my mother!" she said, vehemently. "She couldn't have loved anyone like you, you nutso killer."

"Oh but she did." His voice had changed almost as though he were another person. Maybe he was, she thought. Maybe he was one of those multiple personalities like she had seen on TV. Like in *Sybill*.

He continued. "She wanted to be with me. But then your old man was about to come home and she didn't want to bust up her family." He scowled. "And she pissed me off, you know. She killed our baby. *My* baby!"

Starr's eyes flared. "You're sick, Bobby Zale. *You're* the one that needs to be killed."

His face was sullen, his eyes, frighteningly hollow. "We would have made a nice family, you know. Your mom, you and your little brother or sister. But your old man stood in the way. He didn't have the decency to get himself killed in Vietnam."

"I hate myself for ever liking you. But I hate *you* even more. How could I have been so blind?"

"Just like your mom. She was blind. Blinded by her precious values and conscience. You know what happens to blind people, Starr? They get hurt sometimes, because they can't see. And she refused to see. That's why she's dead. It's *her* fault that I killed her. It's her fault I killed all the others, too."

"You're a despicable bastard," she retorted with as much venom her tongue could spit out.

"Not nice, Starbright. Anyway, I didn't mean to *kill* her. I just wanted to talk to her. I caught up with her on Nine Mile Road and she sped up even more. When we got to the bridge, she hit her brakes and I busted into her. She lost control and went into the water. I watched her sink and then she was gone."

"*You didn't go in to save her?*" Starr's words exploded

in Bobby's face and he flinched. Her teeth and fists were clenched.

Bobby hung his head and dropped the Beretta to his side. "I wanted to, but then I thought if I can't have her, neither can Blake Ravenel." Slowly, calmly, he pulled from the sheath on his belt a knife. Starr knew it had to be the same knife that was used on all the women. Its menacing edge gleamed in the lamplight.

She grabbed the fireplace poker from its stand.

"What do you think you're doing, Starr?" He raised the gun again. "Drop the poker."

She cocked the rod like a baseball bat. "Go ahead, Bobby. You're going to kill me anyway. That's why you're here. But I'll never let you cut me up like you did Marcie Rose."

Bobby took a step toward her and she swung the poker wildly, connecting with the blade. The knife flung out of Bobby's hand across the room and he yelped in pain.

"I didn't want it to end this way, Starr." He then raised the gun again to her head.

Suddenly, there were footsteps on the front porch and then the sound of the doorknob turning. "Starr, are you here? I went by Mrs. Baker's and she wasn't..."

"*Daddy!*" she yelled back. "*He's here! Don't come in!*"

But it was too late. Blake was already entering the hall foyer. As his shadow came into the light, Bobby pivoted and fired twice. The first bullet struck Blake in the thigh, but the second slammed into his chest.

Starr screamed and ran toward her fallen dad. His

hand was still on the grip of his Glock as he lay on the floor beside Burt Morris. Starr bent over her father and sobbed. "Daddy, please don't die."

Blake formed Starr's name on his lips. The light of battle that usually shone in his eyes had faded. Then he closed them. A vision of a high meadow painted with wildflowers of every color entered his brain and then almost immediately it was gone. Instead, what appeared to be a star, moving toward him, piercing the deepest, blackest night, caused him to be lost in its brilliance. He could no longer feel the pain in his chest and leg. His face was the color of bone.

Starr looked up at Bobby who was now standing over them, poised to fire again. "You killed my dad, you bastard!" she sobbed, watching helplessly as her father's life's blood drained out of him.

"I didn't want it to end this way," said Bobby, calmly. "But you wouldn't leave it alone." Pain seemed to grip his face as his index finger tightened around the trigger.

Morris, who had regained consciousness, brought himself to his knees behind Bobby and grabbed his gun hand. The two men wrestled, but Bobby being the stronger, struck Morris in the jaw with his left fist and knocked him into the wall. "Say your prayers, old man," Bobby said, positioning the muzzle within two feet of Morris' head.

The sharp report was deafening and seemed to reverberate throughout the house for several seconds. The bullet tore through Bobby's right temple, splattering blood and brain tissue onto one of the French doors. As his body dropped like a puppet to the floor, Starr, who had secured her father's Glock, maintained her grip on the smoking gun should Bobby twitch a finger. When she was satisfied he wouldn't move again, she laid the Glock down beside her dad and placed her head on his bloodied chest. Suddenly, the door burst open and there stood Linc with gun in hand. Unfortunately, too late.

******

On Monday of the next week a meeting convened in Mayor McCown's office. Present were FBI Special Agents Nelson and Puckett, Agent Lanham, the mayor, of course, and Pine River's acting police chief, Lincoln Ferguson. In fact, Linc *was* Pine River's police force.

McCown initiated the dialogue. "I hate what happened to Blake. God, what an awful year we've had." He folded his hands under his chin in reflection.

Linc nodded. "Yeah, this town's got a lot of healin' to do."

Jim Puckett, stood with coffee and a piece of paper in hand. Always a man of style and dignity, he addressed the group with the eloquence of a William F. Buckley. "Apparently, nobody, not even the Savannah police, did a background check on Robert Zale. It seems in 1973 he moved from here to Savannah, checked himself in a behavioral facility for depression and what is referred to in this summary as 'psychotic episodes.' It says here there were therapist notes indicating that Zale would bring a Raggedy Ann doll to his sessions to use as a prop in his Gestalt role play."

"Yeah," added Linc. "When we went though his garage apartment we found about a dozen of them dolls. We also found a black 1980 Suburban in that garage. Old Bessie Cotter was right after all. Bobby led everyone to believe the patrol car was the only vehicle he had. Guess we got fooled all the way around."

"Easy to be fooled, Chief," said Puckett. "Zale, being a favorite son, high school All-American running back on the high school team, college Criminal Justice major, and ultimately a Savannah detective…who would question the character and background of such a kid?"

Lanham wanted some clarification. "So let me get this straight. After his psycho stay in the hospital in Savannah, I take it he went out west for a couple of years, killed redheads in California and Nevada, *then* came back to Savannah to continue his education and hire on as a Savannah officer?"

"That's correct," chimed in Harm Nelson. "And of course, when he decided to move back to Pine River, that's when Blake and the mayor brought him in here in '78."

Mayor McCown cleared his throat and shuffled his frame around in his leather wingback, seemingly embarrassed that he had something to do with the decision to bring on Bobby Zale.

Lanham again. "We found the Scott woman's hair in the back end of the Suburban. Guess he had sex with her, whether consensual or rape, sliced her up, and then dumped her in the big dumpster behind the Bledsoe woman's house. We still wonder why the dumpster, though? Why not bury her?"

"Maybe he *wanted* her found," replied Nelson. "Maybe he was making a statement to the town, especially to Ravenel. I think he despised and resented the chief all this time, first of all for coming back from the war and then for his wife taking back up with him. That took Zale out of the picture. Zale as much wanted to punish the chief as he did Luann Ravenel for spurning him."

"We also believe all the women except the St. Clair girl entered into a relationship with him," added Puckett. "Ultimately, they figured him out, his abusive and possessive nature, then when they tried to break it off, he likely raped them and cut their throats. His purpose was to humiliate them by exposing their mutilated bodies to the world. And the doll continued to represent the child he lost and could have had with any one of them."

The mayor put up his finger. "And how *about* the St. Clair girl, Agent Puckett?"

"We're not sure, Mayor. Could be since Blake Ravenel was so close to the football coach, Zale killed the girl to cause the chief even more pain. Marcie was like a niece to Blake. She baby-sat Blake's girl over the years, you know. Zale probably figured since Marcie had red hair as well, it would fit the M.O. *and* satisfy his hunger to kill. Anything to cause Blake pain and to relieve his own. And in killing one of the town's precious daughters, the daughter of a true icon, he would also show Blake Ravenel that he could commit murder right under his nose. A kind of 'in your face' deal."

"He must've had a real hard-on about Blake," said McCown. "Funny, I never saw an inkling of such when they were together. I thought they were even buds when off duty. Right, Linc?"

He nodded.

"How is the Baker woman, Mayor?" asked Lanham.

"Recovering. Obviously, Zale wanted to make sure the Ravenel girl didn't get inside Mary Alice's house. That woman's lucky Zale just cracked her on the head and left her for dead. His knife would not have been so forgiving."

"Yeah. Guess since she wasn't a red-head, she didn't merit his blade."

"Hmm. Yes, well, maybe so." The mayor stood as a signal to break up the meeting. It was nine-thirty and he was hungry. "Linc, if I have my way, you'll stay the chief. I guess the council and us will need to take a look at some candidates for the force. But there's one damn thing for sure; we'll be doin' a good background from now on." He smiled to punctuate the statement. "So how about it, boys? Breakfast at the Kudzu? I'll spring."

CHAPTER FIFTEEN

Last night when we were young
Love was a star, a song unsung.
Life was so new, so real, so bright,
Ages ago, last night.

Today, the world is old.
You flew away, and time grew cold.
Where is that star
That seemed so bright
Ages ago, last night.

Arlen/Hapsburg
Carly Simon

On the first Wednesday in October, 2005, a black, unmarked Crown Vic pulled to the edge of the curb in front of a white two-story on Jefferson Street. The driver, FBI Special Agent Starr Ravenel, dropped the sun visor down to put on lipstick. The Bureau frowned on their female agents using more than a touch of make-up, but this was a special day and she wanted to look her best. Before exiting the sedan, she adjusted the Glock on her hip and covered it with her suit jacket.

Even after all these years the old town of Pine River looked pretty much the same. However, the downtown area had died out and laid dormant for years due for the most part to the new mega-mall a couple of miles out of town on the road to Savannah. But in the last three years, civic-minded urbanites had rejuvenated the commercial area of town with yuppie businesses like a gourmet coffee shop and bookstore, two antiques shops and a 'Made-in-Georgia store where *Roy's Toys* used to be. And Tommy Lee Bledsoe was Chief of Police.

Notables had passed on years ago like Mayor McCown, Bennie Griffin, owner of the Kudzu, and the irreplaceable Charlie St. Clair.

Starr rapped a couple of times on the screen door and then stuck her head inside. "Anybody home?"

A small fifty-ish woman with perfectly coiffed blonde hair, showing a bit gray in places, came to the foyer with a dish towel, wiping her hands. "Starr, you're here!" she said gleefully, giving her a hug. "Haven't seen you for over six weeks. I guess the Bureau keeps you hopping."

"More than I'd like, sometimes. You always look so good, Katie. Married life obviously agrees with you."

Katie smiled. Her face, her beautiful lively eyes, and her inviting lips were showing a few lines, but she was still pretty. At fifty-five, she looked ten years younger. Her voice was still sultry, even musical. The brogue, elegantly Southern.

"I stopped by the nursing home to see Mr. Kolb…I still want to call him that…Mr. Morris. Took him his favorite, a box of Russell Stovers."

"How is he? I haven't been by there in six or seven months, I'm sorry to say."

"He seems to be doing all right, I reckon. His mind's not as sharp as it was even a year ago, but he still remembers me. The girl who spied on him. I'll never forget him, Katie. He risked his life to save me."

Starr looked into the kitchen and then scanned the back yard through the window. "Where is he?"

"I think in the shop. No, he's coming in the back door as we speak."

The door opened and the familiar voice shouted, "Starbright!"

"Hi, Dad."

"Ah, you look marvelous, sweetheart. Glad you could make it."

"There's no way I'd miss the twenty year anniversary of my two favorite people in the world. By the way, Dad, I hear you're going to have a great year. Already 4 and 0."

"Yeah, a lot of talent in the squad. We expect Linc's grandson, Marvin, to break the school rushing record. You know last year we had a kid break Bobby's reception….." He stopped short. "Anyway, you are sticking around for Friday's game with Richmond Hill, aren't you?"

"I can't, Dad. But I will be back when you play for

the state championship. I hear you're every bit the icon as Coach St. Clair, now with a state championship already under your belt and making nine regional playoffs."

"I'll never be the football coach the Saint was, Starr. Did you know the town erected a statue of his likeness the other day in the square along with the old Confederate soldier? The difference is that no kid would ever *dare* desecrate Coach's statue like they still do the Johnny Reb. No, Coach has a legacy that will never be equaled."

Starr smiled and hugged Blake again. "Dad, you look good. Lean and handsome as always. How's the leg?"

"It gives me a little trouble from time to time, but get me out on the field with the boys and you'll never know there's a bullet still in there."

"Any breathing problems?"

"Nope. Ribs hurt occasionally during a cold rain. But no worse for wear."

Katie took off her apron and smacked Blake on his rump. "Well, are we ready to go to the Legion Hall or not?"

"Let's do it," answered Blake. "Who all's coming?"

"Tommy Lee should already be there and old Linc is coming up from Tampa with his son. We're expecting over a hundred fifty to help us celebrate. Did we tell you we're also renewing our vows?"

"No. That's neat."

"Before you go back, I want you to take something with you."

"What's that, Dad; the 69 Mach I out there?"

"Not on a bet, Starbright."

"Okay, what?"

"Your telescope has been sitting in that window up there collecting dust all these years, like it's been watching for you to come home. Take it with you, Starr. I know you've got that fancy, high-powered model up there in D.C., but this one was your companion for many years. It knows the Heavens better than any of these new modern scopes. It's waited for you at that window long enough. Time to give it a new home."

CPSIA information can be obtained at www.ICGtesting.com
Printed in the USA
LVOW06s0117031214

416537LV00001B/11/P